"Well, well, well," Avery said. "What do we have here?"

Jennifer raised her hand, palm out. "Stop. Don't say anything that will make me regret coming here more than I already do." She took a deep breath. "Do you still want a riding coach?"

"Maybe."

"If I give you lessons, I need something in return. I need to learn how to use a sword."

"Why ask me?"

She hesitated, then said, "My mother's instructor is unavailable. I called your captain to ask about your unit's saber instructor."

"Which is me."

Her gaze locked with his. "If you're worried our past relationship will get in the way, I can assure you it won't. You want to win the Sheridan Cup. I want to keep my mother's commitment. We can work together to make this happen or we can fail separately. It's up to you."

"No strings attached?"

"None."

Jennifer ignored the nagging little voice that said keeping things businesslike might prove more difficult than expected.

Books by Patricia Davids

Love Inspired

His Bundle of Love
Love Thine Enemy
Prodigal Daughter
The Color of Courage
Military Daddy
A Matter of the Heart
A Military Match

PATRICIA DAVIDS

Patricia Davids continues to work as a part-time nurse in the NICU while writing full-time. She enjoys researching new stories, traveling to new locations and meeting fans along the way. She and her husband of thirty-two years live in Wichita, Kansas, along with the newest addition to the household, a stray cat named Spooky. Pat always enjoys hearing from her readers. You can contact her by mail at P.O. Box 16714, Wichita, Kansas 67216, or visit her on the Web at www.patriciadavids.com.

A Military Match
Patricia Davids

Steeple
Hill®

Published by Steeple Hill Books™

STEEPLE HILL BOOKS

Steeple
Hill®

ISBN-13: 978-0-373-81384-1
ISBN-10:   0-373-81384-8

A MILITARY MATCH

www.SteepleHill.com

Printed in U.S.A.

The horse is made ready for the day of battle,
but victory rests with the Lord.
—*Proverbs* 21:31

This book is dedicated to my brother, Bob Stroda—
a real cowboy and a funny, funny guy. Thanks
for putting up with your bossy big sister and for
making me laugh more times than I can count.

Chapter One

"Stay here...and honk if you see *anyone* going inside."

Jennifer Grant pushed open the door of her old dark blue pickup, but paused to glance at her passenger. "Got it?"

Fifteen-year-old Lizzie Grant, the second of Jennifer's three younger siblings, hooked a lock of curly brown hair behind one ear. She didn't bother looking up from her math book. "I've got it."

"I'm serious." Jennifer stressed each word.

Lizzie shut her book and pulled her pink T-shirt collar up to cover the lower half of her face, mocking her sister's intensity. She glanced in all directions. "Have no fear, Agent Double oh six, Double oh seven is on the job."

"Don't be a smart aleck."

Dropping the fabric, Lizzie opened her book again. "Fine. Then stop acting like a wimp. If I see *Avery,* which is who you're really trying to avoid, I'll honk three times so you'll know your ex-boyfriend is coming."

"Very funny." Jennifer gave her sister a dour look, but knew in her heart that Lizzie was right. Private Avery Barnes was exactly who she wanted to avoid.

"Why do we have to do this now?" Lizzie demanded. "It's Saturday."

"Because Dr. Cutter needs the follow-up films on Dakota's leg done today." *And because Avery should be away from the stable for at least another hour.*

Sighing with teenage impatience, Lizzie focused on her homework once more. "Is it going to take long? I don't want to be late and neither should you."

"It'll take ten minutes, tops. I can get you to your chess meeting, drop the films off at the Large Animal Clinic and still get to my horse show on time."

Jennifer was used to making the most of the limited hours in her day. To save time, she was already dressed in her tan riding breeches and white shirt beneath her pale blue lab coat. Her black show jacket hung in a garment bag behind the driver's seat. Her knee-high riding boots, polished to a high shine, sat ready to be pulled on before she took the field.

After she stepped out of the truck, Jennifer pulled a large yellow case from the front seat and glanced around. The narrow strip of white gravel between the close, single-story stone buildings reflected the heat of the warm September morning. The parking area contained only a few cars, but one was the sleek lapis-blue Jaguar she knew belonged to Avery.

Glancing into the horse trailer hitched behind her truck, she saw McCloud, her gray ten-year-old gelding, standing quietly, his head up and eyes alert. It was a sign he was ready to get down to business. Both of them needed to be on their game today or she would have wasted an entry fee.

Money was tight in the Grant household, and the possibility that she could earn an extra five hundred dollars in prize money wasn't to be taken lightly. Her riding, plus her work for Dr. Cutter, were paying her way though vet school. This semester's fees were due in the next few weeks and she didn't yet have the full amount she needed.

She walked quickly to the wide doorway of the old limestone and timber stable, pausing to check down the dim, cobblestone paved corridor. It was empty. She glanced over her shoulder at a small building a dozen yards away. It housed the offices of the Commanding General's Mounted Color Guard at Fort Riley, Kansas.

No one stepped out to greet her. She relaxed and blew out the breath she had been holding. She had permission to be here, she just didn't want to encounter a certain soldier.

The men who made up Fort Riley's unique cavalry living history unit should be at their training corrals now. When the unit wasn't performing around the country they practiced daily to hone their exceptional equestrian skills and train their horses. She didn't expect anyone back for at least another hour.

Part of her was glad that the maddening Avery Barnes was nowhere in sight. Another part of her half-hoped she'd be able to show him exactly how little she cared if he was. Grasping her equipment case tightly, she walked down the corridor to the last stall on the left.

Inside the old building, the air was cool and laced with the smell of horses, hay and oiled leather. All scents she loved. Opening the upper half of the Dutch door, she spoke softly to the brown horse dozing with his head lowered near the back wall. "Hey, Dakota. What're ya doing?"

When his head came up and she was sure he wasn't startled by her presence, she opened the lower half of the door, stepped inside and held out her hand. Dakota whinnied and came to collect the slice of apple resting in her palm.

She patted his neck as she checked behind her. There was still no one in sight.

"Okay, fella, let's make this quick. I want to get done before you-know-who shows up."

Dropping to her knees, she felt along Dakota's leg, checking for any tenderness or swelling. To her satisfaction she didn't find anything but a nicely healed scar on the big bay's pastern. She popped open the fasteners on the cumbersome yellow case and removed the new portable X-ray machine her boss and mentor, equine surgeon Dr. Brian Cutter, had entrusted her with.

It only took a few minutes to set up and position the machine, and get Dakota to stand with his foot on the X-ray cassette. Taking the series of shots Brian needed to monitor the healing progress of Dakota's fractured leg took only a couple minutes more. She propped one used cassette against the side of the stall behind her so she wouldn't accidentally take two exposures on it, and set up for one final shot.

"Well, well, look who's here. If it isn't my darling Jenny."

As always, the broad New England accent in his deep voice did funny things to the pit of her stomach. Apparently just telling herself she was over him wasn't enough.

When Avery had asked her out the previous winter, Jenny had been flattered but cautious. His playboy reputation was no secret. She'd accepted because she'd sensed that beneath that smooth charm was a lonely man who needed her, and God, in his life.

Getting Avery to open up proved more difficult than she had imagined, but because she cared about him, she hadn't been willing to give up. Jennifer Grant never walked away from a challenge.

In the end, she'd turned to a mutual friend, Lindsey Cutter, for help. Avery and Lindsey had served together in the CGMCG. Lindsey told her that Avery had joined the army after a falling-out with his only remaining family member, his grandfather.

Sensing she had found the key to understanding him, Jennifer had tried repeatedly to talk to Avery about his family, but he shut her out. After wrestling with her conscience, she'd made the decision to contact his grandfather herself. Her good intentions blew up in her face. Avery had found out and had been furious.

Their breakup that day at her clinic was both public and humiliating. Then, as if to prove he'd never really cared about her, Avery spent the next several weeks dating a series of Jenny's classmates.

Which only confirmed that he didn't care about me.

Choosing to ignore her reaction to the sound of his voice, Jennifer snapped the last shot, braced herself, then rose to face him.

Lizzie was in so much trouble. A heads-up really would have been nice.

Leaning with his tan forearms resting on the half door, he grinned at her with a cocky smile that had probably melted more female hearts than she could count. It had certainly softened hers the first time she saw it. Fortunately, she knew him better now. *Un*fortunately, the lesson had been an emotionally painful one to learn.

He wore the unit's standard issue red T-shirt. His matching red ball cap was pushed back on his head revealing his military-cut dark brown hair above his deep-set hazel eyes.

Eyes that a woman could get lost in—if she didn't have the good sense to see Avery Barnes for what he was—a playboy who broke hearts without a second thought.

"I'm not *your* anything, Private Barnes, and you know that I don't like being called Jenny."

It had taken months, but she had patched her heart back together with will power and hard work. She wasn't about to let him think she still cared. She didn't. She was *so* over him.

"It's Corporal Barnes now. I've been promoted since we last met and now that you mention it, Jenny, I do recall that you don't like being called Jenny."

"I'm busy. Go away if you can't be nice." She imbued her voice with as much toughness as she could muster.

A second soldier came up to stand beside Avery. Jennifer recognized another member of the mounted color guard. Private Lee Gillis was dressed in the same red shirt with the unit's logo embroidered on it. His smile, unlike Avery's, showed genuine warmth.

"Hi, Jennifer," Lee said brightly. "What are you doing here? I thought you'd be riding in the Deerfield Open today."

Lee, like many soldiers assigned to the CGMCG, had never been on a horse before his transfer into the special unit a year ago. Everyone who came into the unit trained in cavalry tactic from manuals the U.S. Army had used during the Civil War. Once exposed to the world of equestrian sports, Lee had quickly become a fan of all things horse related, particularly show jumping and dressage. Jennifer often saw him at the local events when she was competing.

"Yes, Jenny, what are you doing here?" Avery interjected with mock interest. "Besides looking for me."

"I have absolutely no interest in seeing you. Dr. Cutter sent me to take Dakota's follow up films this month and if you call me Jenny one more time, I'm going to make you regret it."

Avery shook his head as he gave her a reproachful look. "Shame on you—threatening a member of the U.S. military. I could get you in serious trouble for that."

Jennifer smiled at Lee. "You'll short sheet his bed or put a large snake in it for me, won't you?"

Lee's eyes brightened. "Gladly."

Folding her arms over her chest, she said, "You see, Avery, I can get to you whenever I want."

"Lee, do you know why she doesn't like to be called Jenny?"

Holding up both hands, Lee took a step back. "I think you two should leave me out of this."

"Because a jenny is a female donkey," Avery said with a smirk. "Can you see the resemblance? Cute, with big ears and a long nose that gets into everyone's business, and too stubborn for her own good—that's my Jenny in a nutshell."

"I didn't come here to be abused by you. I'm here to do a job and you're interfering. Do I need to tell Captain Watson that you're ignoring your own work and keeping me from doing mine? I'm sure it won't be the first time he's heard that you're slacking."

"She's got you there, Avery." Grinning, Lee slapped his buddy on the back then walked away.

"You can tattle to the captain if it makes you feel better, Jenny, but the truth is I'm not doing a thing to prevent you from working. I'm just standing here watching."

Jennifer bit back a retort. The last thing she wanted was to get into a verbal battle with the man. Instead, she turned away and stuffed the X-ray machine into the carrying case before snapping it shut. "I'm finished anyway."

Picking up the case, she spun around and marched toward the stall door. Avery pulled it open, swept his arm out and bowed low in a courtly gesture as she passed. She wasn't sure, but she thought she heard him chuckling behind her.

The man was insufferable. Why she had ever considered him handsome and interesting was a complete mystery.

The bright sunshine made her squint after the

dimness of the barn's interior. She shaded her eyes with one hand as she crossed to her truck and yanked open the door. After depositing the equipment inside, she slid behind the wheel.

"Thanks a lot, Lizzie. I thought I told you to honk if you saw anyone coming."

Tapping her lips with her pencil, Lizzie frowned at her book. "I didn't see anyone."

Jennifer took a few deep breaths before inserting her key in the ignition. "Dr. Cutter is just going to have to get one of his other students to come do these films."

"Didn't you volunteer to do them?" Lizzie scowled as she wrote in her notebook.

"I did, but good grades are only worth so much aggravation."

"Oh, *he* was there." Lizzie turned the page and copied a set of numbers on her paper.

"I could care less about Avery Barnes," Jennifer stated firmly, hoping to convince herself as much as her sister.

"You were drooling over him last winter when the army had Dakota at your clinic."

"I don't recall drooling over anyone."

"You went out with him last winter and every other word out of your mouth was Avery this and Avery that and Avery is so charming."

Jennifer still wasn't certain how she could

have been so mistaken about him. Her first impression had been that Avery was devoted to his friends and to helping care for injured animals. Both were qualities she greatly admired. She had sensed something special in him. She had begun to see a future with him.

A future, as it turns out, based on foolish daydreams with no basis in reality.

"He's charming all right. He's also as shallow as a petri dish. We saw each other for a few months, but then I learned how superficial and self-centered he really is."

"Why? Because he stopped asking you out?"

Her sister's comment hit a little too close to home. "I'm not having this conversation with you."

Rolling her eyes, Lizzie said, "Whatever. If we don't get going, I'll be late for my chess club."

Jennifer started the engine and checked her rearview mirror as she pulled away from the stable, but she wasn't granted another glimpse of the unbearable Avery Barnes. Which was just as well, she decided as she headed toward the checkpoint at the east entrance of the post. If she never had to see him again, it would be too soon.

Chapter Two

As Avery listened to the sound of Jennifer's truck driving away, he tried to ignore the ache in the back of his throat. He rubbed his hands on the sides of his jeans and hoped the fact that she still took his breath away had gone unnoticed. Acting like a jerk wasn't usually so hard.

He hadn't expected to see her again after the painful brush off he'd given her. Certainly not here in his company's stable. The harshness of his behavior after their breakup pricked what little conscience he had left, but he tried to ignore that, too.

He thought he'd put his feelings for her behind him. Now, standing here with the lingering scent of her perfume filling him with warmth, he knew he hadn't. It had been a long time since a woman had affected his equilibrium the way Jennifer Grant did.

It wasn't that she was such a knockout in the looks department. She wasn't overly tall, but she had a trim figure and a self-assured way of tossing her blond hair back with a flip of her hand that made a man sit up and take notice. Her nose had a little bump in the middle that the women in his circles would have had smoothed out by a plastic surgeon before they finished high school.

Jennifer's appeal wasn't in her deep blue eyes or in her looks. It was how she looked at others. Her kindness and her compassion lit her from the inside like a candle in the darkness. She was unlike anyone he had ever met. The only trouble with Jennifer was that she never knew when to quit.

His first reaction when he saw her today in Dakota's stall had been a surge of happiness. He was thankful her back had been turned and he'd had time to school his features into a smirk he knew would annoy her.

What he should have done was keep walking and let her leave without speaking to her. Even now he wasn't sure why he'd felt compelled to engage her in conversation. He knew she wouldn't have anything nice to say to him.

Perhaps he had been hoping for a tongue lashing from her. Maybe he even had it coming.

Dakota thrust his head out the stall door and whinnied after Jennifer. Avery reached up to scratch the horse behind his ear. "Sorry I ran her off, big boy. I know you like her."

Dakota had gone through a rough time after his fracture the previous autumn. For a while, it had looked like the horse wouldn't survive. Jennifer had been one of the people involved in his care, and his recovery was due in part to the hours she spent helping take care of him.

Avery remembered Dakota's stay at the Large Animal Clinic with more fondness than the circumstances warranted. It had been Jennifer's company, her upbeat attitude and her bossy but kind nature that had helped everyone from the mounted color guard cope during those difficult days.

It was only later that Avery had realized what a danger she posed to his peace of mind. She was far too likable—and good. Definitely not what he looked for in the women he dated.

He patted Dakota's neck. "If she wasn't so cute when she gets mad I might have been able to stop egging her on. Did you see the way that fire leaps in those deep blue eyes?" Giving himself a mental shake for discussing Jennifer with a horse, Avery walked on toward the equipment room.

Lee came out of the door with two long-handled pitchforks and handed one to Avery. It was their turn to muck out the stalls before the rest of the unit returned from exercising the horses.

"Why do you razz Jennifer like that?" Lee asked as he pushed a wheelbarrow toward the first empty stall.

Avery wasn't in the habit of sharing his feelings or explaining his actions. He shrugged. "She can take it."

"And dish it out, but you seem to take a special delight in ruffling her feathers. What did she ever do to you?"

"Nothing."

"I seem to remember that the two of you had a thing going for a while. What happened?"

"We went out a couple of times. It didn't work." Avery began pitching the straw from the first stall into the wheelbarrow.

Lee stopped and grinned at him. "She dumped you."

"Get real. Women don't dump me."

Only one had. After that, he never gave another woman the chance. He was always the first to call it quits in a relationship.

"Jennifer didn't fall for your smooth-talking ways, did she? That must have bruised your ego."

"My ego is unscathed, thank you. It just so happens the woman can't leave well enough alone."

"What does that mean?"

"She wanted me to go to church with her."

Lee resumed his work. "I go to church. It wouldn't hurt you to give it a try."

"Believing that someone or something is in charge of my life doesn't do it for me. Anyway, she didn't stop there. After I turned her down and expressed my views on the subject, she made a point of telling all the women at the clinic to steer clear of me."

"So that's what the big ears and long nose comment was about?"

"She thinks she knows what's best for everyone." She thought she knew what was best for him.

"I heard she was the one who got Dr. Cutter and Lindsey Mandel to patch things up. Now look at them."

"Exactly. They're married. In a year they'll both be miserable and filing for divorce because they hate each other."

Lee paused and leaned on his pitchfork. "Not every marriage ends in misery."

"Enough do. If flying in a plane was as risky as marriage, nobody would be racking up frequent flyer miles."

One look at his parents' marriage and his own near miss proved his point.

"That's a grim view."

"I call it like I see it."

"I wonder if that's true." Lee propped his pitchfork against the wall and lifted the handles of the wheelbarrow.

Avery looked at him sharply. "What does that mean?"

"It means you might not want to admit it, but you've still got a thing for Jennifer." Lee maneuvered the loaded cart out the doorway, leaving Avery to stare after him.

Jennifer pulled up in front of the youth center at the Community Christian Church and checked her watch. "See, I told you I'd get you here on time. Is your math done? You know I'm not going to let you shirk your school work just to have a wild time with your chess-loving friends."

Lizzie scribbled one more number on her sheet and snapped the textbook shut. "I'm done."

"Okay, but I still need to check it before I turn you loose."

Handing over her work, Lizzie said, "Like that's a surprise. You're way stricter than Mom is."

"That's because, unlike our mother, I believe your education is more important than a silly hobby."

As soon as the words were out of her mouth, Jennifer's conscience pricked her. She shouldn't be criticizing her mother's behavior, or calling her sister's hobby silly.

Still, Mary Grant's obsession with history and re-enacting the life of frontier widow Henrietta Dutton had been taking up more and more of her time. Her involvement with the local historical society's plans for the town's upcoming Founder's Day Festival had turned into a time-consuming passion that left all of her kids feeling ignored.

There were times when Jennifer wondered if the line between reality and re-enactment were blurring a bit too much even for their eccentric mother.

"Your horse shows are a hobby," Lizzie said defensively.

"Yes, they are, but I don't let them interfere with my education or my job."

Someone in the family had to keep a level head. Since her father's death eight years ago, that lot had fallen to Jennifer. It wasn't that she resented it, because she did love her family, but there were times when she felt stifled in responsibility.

She glanced at her sister's downcast face and realized that she had sounded much too stern. Reaching over, she playfully tweaked Lizzie's nose. "Only God and shoe shopping are more important. Right?"

Jennifer was rewarded with the smile she had been hoping for. Lizzie rolled her eyes and shook her head. "Whatever. Is my math right?"

Jennifer checked it. "As usual, it's perfect. Go on and have a good time."

Lizzie pushed open her door, hopped out and slung her tattered black backpack over one shoulder. "Bobby Pinkerton has been telling everyone he's going to beat me in fifteen moves. I can't wait to make him eat his words."

Jennifer grinned. "You go, girl. Trounce that boy."

"I will. I hope you and McCloud win today, too."

"If we do, I'll get pizza for supper. Mom is picking you up, right?"

"Yup. I told her four o'clock."

A teenage girl came racing across the parking lot and Jennifer recognized her as one of Lizzie's friends. Slamming the door shut, Lizzie hurried toward her friend and the two of them entered the building.

After dropping her sister off, Jennifer drove a few more miles to the Kansas State University campus. The Large Animal Clinic was part of the Veterinary Teaching Hospital and Jennifer's boss, Dr. Brian Cutter, was the chief equine surgeon at the facility.

She parked her truck and trailer at the side of the building. Getting out, she turned and grabbed the X-ray machine. The second she did, she realized her mistake.

"Oh, I can't believe it!" She stamped her foot in sheer frustration.

"What's wrong, Jennifer?"

She whirled around to see Brian coming out of the building. Dressed in his usual dark slacks and pristine white lab coat, he leaned heavily on his cane as he walked toward her. Under his arm, he held a small, tan pet carrier.

Jennifer's shoulders slumped as she admitted her mistake. "I took the films you wanted of Dakota's leg, but I left one of the cassettes in his stall. Can you send someone else to get it?"

"It's Saturday. No one is in today except Deborah and I, and of course, Isabella." He nodded toward the crate under his arm where his pet rabbit rested, her nose pressed against the cage door and quivering with excitement.

The brown French lop was a favorite with everyone who worked at the clinic. She had the run of Brian's office plus a small enclosed pen outside the building where she happily napped in the shade or nibbled grass. It was well known that she had her owner and half the staff wrapped around her dainty paw.

Jennifer sighed. "I'm going to go out on a limb here and guess that Isabella doesn't have a driver's license."

He grinned. "Not even a learner's permit."

"And if an emergency came in they would need you and you need Deborah to answer the phone and check people in, so that leaves me to make the trip back to the fort. Are you sure you need the films today?"

"Very sure. My grant money depends on accurate and up-to-date information on the results of my gene therapy subjects. The bone growth study Dakota is part of is one of my most important projects. I wouldn't ask you to make another trip to the fort if I didn't need it today. Do you want me to call and see if they have someone who can bring it over?"

Jennifer checked her watch and blew her breath out through pursed lips. She didn't want to miss her competition, but she didn't want Avery doing her work for her. "No, I'll go back."

"Before you leave, I wanted to ask if you could rabbit-sit for a few days. Well, actually a week. Lindsey and I are going out of town and I know how much you like Isabella. We'd pay you the same as last time."

"I'd be happy to watch her." Every extra dime helped, but Jennifer would have done it for free.

"Great." He deposited Isabella in her run and took the X-ray case from Jennifer. "I'm sorry you have to make a second trip to the post. This won't make you miss your show, will it?"

"No, I can still get there." She smiled but it took more effort than usual.

Getting back into her truck, she made a tight turn and sped out of the parking lot back toward the fort. If she picked up the film and got back in thirty minutes, she could still make her events, but it wouldn't leave her much time to warm up McCloud. The show jumping would be first with the more intricate dressage class scheduled for the afternoon. If she missed the first event she could still enter the later one, but only the horse and rider with the best overall score in both classes would win the top prize money being offered.

It was money she sorely needed. Both her

younger brothers had outgrown last year's school clothes and she had noticed Lizzie's backpack was falling apart. Every extra bit of cash came in handy to help her mother support a family of four children and two horses.

Ten minutes later, Jennifer stopped at the gates of the fort to hand over her identification. As she waited for permission to enter, she mentally braced herself to face Avery again. Having to admit he had rattled her enough to make her forget her job was a sobering thought.

After being waved through the checkpoint, she quickly drove to the stables and parked beside them. She got out of her truck just as a black limousine drove up and stopped in front of the CGMCG office building. A chauffeur in a dark blue uniform stepped out and moved to open the door for his passenger. A white-haired man in a beautifully tailored gray pinstriped suit emerged.

Distinguished was the first word that popped into Jennifer's mind when she saw him. Money was the second word.

She tilted her head as she studied him. There was something familiar about him, but he entered the office building before she could place where she might have seen him before.

It didn't matter. What mattered was getting

her job done and getting to her contest on time. She got out of her vehicle and walked boldly into the stable all the while praying she wouldn't run into Avery again.

Reaching Dakota's stall without meeting anyone, she opened the door and stepped inside, speaking softly to the big bay who had his nose buried in his feed bucket. The X-ray film cassette was exactly where she had left it leaning against the wall. Snatching it up, she turned and started toward the door when she heard someone call Avery's name.

"Coming," he shouted back. He was just outside.

Without thinking, Jennifer dropped into a crouch behind the half door. He must have been in the tack room on the other side of the walkway. She heard the creak of the door and his boots on the stone floor, but they didn't pass by. They stopped right outside Dakota's stall.

Jennifer closed her eyes and let her chin drop onto her chest. Realizing just what a ridiculous position she had placed herself in, she tried to think of a way to exit with her dignity intact but couldn't come up with anything.

"What are you doing here?" Avery demanded with cool disdain.

Chapter Three

Jennifer looked up expecting to see Avery glaring at her over the stall door, but the space above her was empty. He wasn't talking to her.

"Can't I pay my only grandson a visit?"

It was Avery's grandfather. The man Jennifer had tried and failed to contact. His dragon of a secretary had refused to put Jennifer's call through the day she'd attempted to call.

"I don't have anything to say to you. Did *she* put you up to this?" Avery's cold tone made Jennifer cringe.

Great! He's going to blame me, anyway.

"I don't know who you're talking about. No one put me up to this. Coming here was my own idea. Can't we at least try to let bygones be bygones?"

"Why should I?"

"I thought perhaps you would have seen the error of your ways by now."

"I knew you didn't come to apologize."

"I have nothing to apologize for. I was protecting you. You would see that if you opened your eyes."

Jennifer pressed a hand to her mouth. Her foolish pride had placed her in the awkward position of eavesdropping on a family quarrel. There was no other way out of the stall. She braced herself to stand up and let them know she was there when Avery's next words stopped her.

"I don't have to stay and listen to this."

Jennifer heard his footsteps moving away and she breathed a sigh of relief. She just might get out of this with her dignity intact.

"She didn't love you. All she cared about was your money," Avery's grandfather called out loudly.

"No, all *you* ever cared about was money," Avery shot back.

"It never bothered you to spend the money I earn," the older man answered sharply. "You never had to work for anything…and that was my fault as much as anyone's."

"What you really mean is that I'll never amount to anything. I've heard this speech before."

"I have been guilty of saying that in the past,

that's true, but I simply wanted you to stop wasting your life."

"It's my life. Which is something you never understood."

Dakota had finished his meal and walked over to Jennifer. He nickered softly and nuzzled at her pocket. She pushed his head away. He gave a loud snort and she tensed. He snorted again and whinnied.

"Shh," she whispered with her fingertips pressed to her lips, hoping to quiet him and praying the men wouldn't notice anything unusual.

"Thanks for the visit, Grandfather. I'm sure you can find your own way out." Avery's voice drifted to her from the front of the barn and she knew he had walked away.

"Wait!" the older man called out. "I didn't mean for this to become one of our shouting matches. Please come back."

There was no answer. Jennifer heard his heavy sigh, then his unsteady footsteps faded, too.

A wave of sympathy engulfed her. How terribly sad for both men. Avery had always avoided talking about his family except to tell her that his parents were dead. He had never mentioned his grandfather. Now she knew why.

Rising, she opened the stall door and stepped

out. A few feet away, the elderly man from the limousine sat on a bale of straw. His eyes opened wide at the sight of her.

Heat rushed to her cheeks. "I'm so sorry," she stammered. "I didn't mean to, but I couldn't help…overhearing."

He closed his eyes and waved his hand. "It doesn't matter. I've lost him. He's all I have and he hates me."

The resignation and pain in his voice touched her deeply.

"You mustn't think that. There is always a chance for reconciliation."

He shook his head. "You don't know all that stands between us."

She took a step closer. "You're right. I don't, but I do know that faith is a powerful tool. Faith and hard work can overcome the most insurmountable problems."

"Wise advice from someone so young, but my grandson isn't the forgiving kind."

The old man tried to rise to his feet, but sat down abruptly with his hand pressed to his chest. Beads of sweat popped out on his forehead and his face grew bright red. She dropped to her knees in front of him. "Are you okay?"

Nodding, he fumbled at the breast pocket of his jacket. He pulled out a small, dark glass bottle but couldn't hold on to it. It tumbled from his trembling hand. Jennifer caught it before it hit the stone floor.

A quick glance at the prescription label confirmed her suspicions. It was heart medication.

She opened the cap and shook one tiny white tablet onto her palm. Pinching it between her thumb and forefinger, she held it out to him. "Put this under your tongue."

He nodded, took the pill from her and put it in his mouth. She closed her hand around his wrist to check his pulse. It was fast, but not irregular. "I'm going to call 9-1-1."

He managed a tight smile. "No. The medicine will help. I don't need an ambulance."

"Shall I get Avery?"

Shaking his head, he said, "I don't want him to see me like this."

"Sir, you aren't well. You grandson should know that."

"I'm fine now."

Although she was relieved to see his color returning to normal and his voice growing stronger, his statement didn't fool her. "Not to be disrespectful, sir, but you are not fine. Those pills are for angina. If you are having heart pain, you need to see a doctor, ASAP."

"I thought perhaps I was talking to one."

"Me? I'm a veterinary student. Give me a lame horse and I can help, but I don't treat people."

"That is a pity." He patted her hand. "You have an excellent bedside manner and you're much prettier than the crusty old fellow who treats me."

She relaxed a fraction and smiled at his teasing. "Flattery—while always deeply appreciated—will get you nowhere."

"I really am feeling better. As you must have heard, I'm Avery's grandfather. My name is Edmond Barnes. I don't believe I caught your name, young lady."

"Pleased to meet you, Mr. Barnes. I'm Jennifer Grant and I should still call an ambulance."

He rose to his feet. "I'll simply refuse treatment."

Rising, she planted her hands on her hips. "When I first saw you I thought I noticed something familiar. Now I see the resemblance. You and Avery share the same strong chin, the same eyes and the same hole in your head where your common sense belongs."

He chuckled. "You must have more than a passing acquaintance with my grandson."

Heat rose in her cheeks. "We've met," she admitted.

Edmond studied her intently. "What do you think of him?"

His question caught her off guard. Should she tell the truth, or amend it to make a sick old man feel better? She didn't want to do either. "Perhaps you should ask his commanding officer that question."

"I'm asking you."

"Avery and I don't exactly see eye-to-eye on things," she admitted slowly. "Sometimes, I think he is his own worst enemy."

"That's very astute." Edmond began walking toward the stable door. Jennifer took his elbow to steady him. When they reached his car, his driver got out and opened the door for him.

Edmond paused, but glanced back at her and said, "When I was a young man, I started a small real estate firm. Over my lifetime I turned it into a multi-million dollar corporation. I learned to read people well and quickly because I had to, but I've never been able to tell what Avery is thinking."

Jennifer hesitated, then found herself saying, "You shouldn't give up on him."

Where had that come from? She was the last person who should be sticking up for Avery.

"I'll admit things didn't go well today, but thanks to my crusty doctor and a triple bypass surgery, I've been given the chance to make things right. I'm not giving up on my grandson. I'll find a way to reach him."

She smiled. "Good."

"Thank you again for your kindness, Miss Grant."

After he drove away, Jennifer glanced at her watch. If she left right now she might just make the first round of jumping at the Deerfield Open. Even though she knew she should leave, she found herself staring toward the Commanding General's Mounted Color Guard office.

Edmond Barnes was a sick man who wanted to reconcile with his grandson. Could she help? Had God placed her here today for that reason? If it were only Avery's feelings to consider she might drive off without a backward glance. She bit her lip in indecision.

As if summoned by her thoughts of him, the office door opened and Avery stepped out into the sunshine. "I saw your truck was here again. Where were you? Hiding in the hay loft?"

"I forgot an X-ray film in Dakota's stall. Avery, I honestly had nothing to do with his coming here."

"A likely story. Just admit you can't stay away from me, Jenny."

She struggled with her rising indignation. Why did he have to turn everything into a joke? "Trust you to kill any kindness I might be feeling."

"Kindness? Don't tell me that manipulative old man made you feel sorry for me? Does he want you to help us patch things up?"

"Would that be such a bad thing?"

A shadow flickered in his eyes and she understood what Edmond had meant about not being able to read him.

"Careful, Jenny. Your nose is cute but it doesn't belong in my business." The edge in his voice should have been enough to send her on her way, but for some reason it wasn't.

"Our families are an important part of who we are. You shouldn't dismiss him out of hand. Forgiveness heals the forgiver as well as the forgiven."

"Shame on you for eavesdropping."

Heat rushed to her cheeks. She folded her arms across her chest. "I wasn't eavesdropping. I accidentally overheard part of your conversation," she conceded.

Raising one eyebrow, he asked, "How is that not eavesdropping?"

She glanced down at the toe of her work boot. "Okay, I'm sorry I didn't let you know I was in Dakota's stall."

"Skip it, Jennifer. It doesn't matter." There was a touch of defeat in his tone.

She looked up and met his gaze. "I honestly didn't mean to listen in on a private family matter. I am sorry."

A smile twitched at the corner of his mouth. "I can't believe I lived to see the day Miss Jenny Grant acknowledged a fault. I'm going to have to mark this on my calendar."

Raising her chin a notch higher, she countered, "Unlike some people I know, I can admit when I'm wrong."

"Unlike some people I know, I mind my own business."

She touched a finger to her lips as she pressed them together, then pointed at him. "You know what? You're right. It's none of my business if you shun your own family, but in the end, you are the one who is going to suffer."

The sound of horses approaching at a rapid trot heralded the return of the troop. Avery took a step closer to her. "Do you charge for your advice, Dr. Jenny? I hope not, because it isn't worth anything."

Jennifer drew a deep breath to keep from making another comment. No matter what she said, he would always find a way to have the last word at her expense.

She spun on her heels and marched to her truck. Trying to help Avery had been a total waste of time.

Avery started to go after Jennifer and apologize, but stopped himself. It was better to let her believe he was a complete jerk. That way she wouldn't be tempted to interfere again. She was better off staying out of his family feud. His grandfather might pass himself off as a caring old man, but Avery knew better.

Edmond wasn't above using anyone or anything to gain the upper hand. He had certainly proved that to Avery beyond a shadow of a doubt.

Yet the old man still possessed the ability to make Avery feel worthless and insignificant.

No one could live up to the expectations his grandfather had set. Avery had given up trying years ago. It wasn't until he saw his grandfather again today that Avery realized he still cared what Edmond thought of him.

As the column of riders approached the stable yard, a jeep stopped on the roadway in front of them and a young corporal got out. Captain Watson reined his horse to a halt beside him as the rest of the unit continued on. The corporal saluted, handed the captain a thick envelope, then jumped in the jeep and drove off.

The previously quiet stable became a hive of activity around Avery as the group dismounted and led their animals into their stalls. The men's jovial chatter, the eager nickering of hungry mounts and the clatter of iron shod hooves on the old cobblestone floors brought the stable to life as it had for more than a century.

Although Avery would never admit it out loud, he was proud of his part in keeping the cavalry's heritage alive. He loved the unit and all it stood for. The army had been good to him.

Captain Watson rode up, dismounted and handed the reins to Avery. "Tell the men to gather in the ready room. We have new orders."

"Yes, sir." Avery saluted and led the captain's horse into the barn where he passed the word, then rubbed down and stabled the captain's mount.

Twenty minutes later, the sixteen soldiers of the Commanding General's Mounted Color Guard were seated in gray folding chairs in a small meeting room at one end of the barn. They rose to their feet when Captain Watson walked in.

"Take your seats, men. As most of you know, the American Cavalry Competition is being held at Fort Riley this year and we've just received permission to participate."

A cheer went up from the group. Grinning, the captain motioned for silence. "We also have three major performances scheduled during the next few weeks. That means a lot of travel for some of you, but I'm confident that this year we're going to bring the Sheridan's Cup back where it belongs. To the home of America's cavalry!"

Avery observed the buzz of excitement in the group with mild amusement. The chance for the CGMCG to showcase their skills and outshine the unit that had won last year's contest had them trash-talking like a pumped up high school football squad.

"Okay, men," the captain continued. "This isn't just about beating the socks off the Fort Humphrey boys. We'll be facing police mounted units, National Guard mounted units and quite a few re-enactor units in the Platoon Drill event.

"All of you are free to enter the individual riding classes. They include Mounted Saber, Mounted Pistol, Military Horsemanship and Military Field Jumping. A plaque will also be awarded for the outstanding horse at the competition."

"It should go to Dakota," Lee suggested.

Captain Watson smiled. "Dakota has certainly earned a special place in this unit, but I'm not sure he is up to performing at such a high level. Dr. Cutter will give us his opinion on that soon."

Avery had been riding Dakota in the various

parades and performances where jumping and rapid stops weren't required, but he suspected the horse was strong enough to compete.

Shuffling through the papers in his hand, the captain found the one he was seeking. "Winners of the individual events will be invited to compete in a combination test of skills for the Sheridan Cup. Besides the silver trophy and a one thousand dollar cash prize, the winner will have his name added to the bronze plaque displayed in the U.S. Cavalry Memorial Research Library. I don't need to tell you that Command is hoping it will be a Fort Riley soldier this year."

Captain passed out the entry forms to the men crowding around him and then dismissed the group. Avery rose and left the building. He had just reached his car when he heard Captain Watson call his name. Turning, he saw his commander approaching holding out a sheet of paper. "Aren't you going to enter?"

"I wasn't planning on it."

The captain pressed his lips together and frowned. "The Sheridan Cup carries a lot of prestige for the brass here. You are better than anyone I've ever seen with a saber and just as good as most with a pistol. I think you could win."

Taken aback by the praise, Avery found himself at a loss for words. In the back of his mind he heard his grandfather's voice telling him he'd never amount to anything. Yet here was his captain, a man he admired, telling him he believed he could win the most coveted prize in the modern cavalry.

"I can't order you to enter the individual classes," the captain continued, "but I'm asking you to do it for the honor of this company."

What if he entered and failed to win?

His grandfather would expect him to fail.

According to him, I fail at everything except spending money. So why do I still care what he thinks? I'm not a failure.

He did care what his captain and the men in the unit thought of him. Could he face disappointing them? "I'll think about it, sir."

"Let me know by tomorrow. Dakota is assigned to you, but you can pick another horse for the competition if Dr. Cutter doesn't think Dakota should participate."

Lee, who had been waiting nearby, came over after the captain walked away. "Are you going to enter?"

"I said I'd think about it."

"You can enter, but don't plan on winning."

Avery cocked his head to the side. "And why is that?"

"I've seen a couple of the riders from the

National Guard Volunteers in action. You'll be outclassed."

"You just heard the captain say that I'm the best he's ever seen with a saber."

"Oh, I agree, but that's only a quarter of the overall score. You might be as good with a pistol as those boys, but they'll ride you into the dirt in Military Horsemanship. That's like dressage and no offence, but you stink at that."

"Okay, my fancy riding could use some work. You seem to know so much about it, why don't you give me a few lessons?"

"Me? I'm worse than you are. You need someone who really knows how to work with you and your horse."

Avery glanced at the men leaving the building. "So which of the guys in the unit is better?"

Lee shoved his hands in his pockets. "I hate to say it, but most of us are pretty average."

Exasperated, Avery said, "All right, you go to horse shows all the time. Who's the best in this area? Who can I get a few pointers from?"

Lee burst out laughing.

Avery scowled at him. "What's so funny?"

Controlling his mirth with difficulty, Lee managed to say, "Jennifer Grant is the best dressage rider in the area, but from what I've seen, she isn't going to give *you* the time of day."

Chapter Four

It was almost dark by the time Jennifer turned into the gravel drive that led to her family's double-wide mobile home on their twenty acres outside Dutton. To her relief she saw her mother's green-and-white pickup and horse trailer sitting in front of their small barn. She had been half afraid that her mother wouldn't be home yet.

The front stoop light came on and Lizzie, followed by twelve-year-old Toby and eight-year-old Ryan, piled out of the door to race toward her. She stopped beside the chain link fence that surrounded their tiny overgrown yard and rolled down her window.

"I smell pizza," Toby shouted as he pulled open the gate.

Picking up the warm cardboard box from the

seat beside her, Jennifer passed it out the window to her eager siblings.

Lizzie took the box, holding it over her head to keep Toby from grabbing it. "I told you she would win."

Toby snatched the box from his sister's hand. "I hope it's pepperoni."

Lizzie snatched it back. "I hope it's cheese."

"Be careful or it will be a dirt pizza," Jennifer warned, but the two of them were already on their way into the house.

Ryan, the youngest and quietest of the Grant kids, looked up at Jennifer. "Did you win?"

She gave him a tired smile. "I won the dressage class."

"But not the jumping class?"

"No."

"Why? Did McCloud miss some jumps?"

"I wish I could blame him, but the truth is, I didn't get there in time to enter."

"Oh." He shoved his hands in the pocket of his jeans and kicked at a bit of gravel with the toe of his shoe. "I guess that means you didn't win enough to get me a new bike."

"No. I'm sorry, sweetheart. I only won enough to cover the money I spent to enter, the pizza and feed for the horses." Jennifer stepped out and began walking to the back of the trailer.

Ryan followed her. "That's okay. I don't really need it. It's almost winter anyway."

She wanted to hug him, but she knew he wouldn't appreciate the gesture. He hadn't been able to go dirt bike riding with his friends since their mother had accidentally run over his bicycle. Jennifer knew he missed hanging out with his buddies, but there were so many other things the family needed first.

"You should go inside before your brother eats your slices of pizza."

"I'm not hungry. Can I help you put your stuff away?"

"Sure. You get the saddle and pad and I'll take McCloud. I almost forgot to mention that Dr. Cutter has asked me to keep Isabella for a few day."

His eyes lit up. "Really? That's great. She's a cool rabbit, but won't Mom be upset? She got kind of mad when Isabella was here last time."

He stood aside as Jennifer backed her horse out of the trailer. "Mom was just upset because Isabella liked to run in and out of her long skirts and chew on the lace. We'll keep Isabella in her cage when Mom is in one of her costumes."

"Maybe we should keep her in the barn."

Jennifer stopped and looked down at him. "Mom or the rabbit?"

Ryan's mouth fell open, then he started to laugh and Jennifer grinned, too.

Ten minutes later, they finished putting McCloud out into the pasture with Lollypop, their mother's black mare. The two horses greeted each other with soft whinnies. Soon they moved off and began grazing together as the last golden rays of sunlight faded from the western sky.

When Jennifer and Ryan entered the house, she sent him to wash up. Lizzie and Toby were sitting on the worn blue sofa in front of the TV. The pizza box, with two small slices remaining, sat open on the kitchen table.

Jennifer washed up at the kitchen sink, then put both slices in the microwave. When Ryan returned, she handed him the plate and a glass of milk. He took it and joined his brother and sister on the couch.

Jennifer settled for a glass of milk and the last apple in the vegetable drawer. After tossing the empty pizza box in the trash, she retrieved her textbooks from her room and returned to the table to study.

A few minutes later, Jennifer looked up as Mary Grant came out of her bedroom and entered the kitchen. Her mother was wearing one of her 1850s-style dresses, a deep blue and white plaid cotton dress with a full skirt over layers of white petticoats.

"Oh, good, you're home," Mary said, turning around. "Can you hook me?"

"Are you going out like that?"

"The historical society is meeting at the Dutton mansion in Old Towne tonight."

"So?" Old Towne was a collection of log cabins, restored businesses and homes from the early 1850s. The Dutton mansion was a simple two-story house with pretentious white columns supporting a small balcony across the front of the building. It was the town historical society's fondest hope that they could turn the area into a profitable tourist attraction.

"Really, Jennifer. You know as an employee of Old Towne I can't go onto the property unless I'm in period dress. I am, after all, Henrietta Dutton. I'm not about to greet visitors to my home in anything but my freshest gown."

Jennifer tugged on the tight bodice and began fastening the long row of hooks down the back of the garment. "It seems kind of silly to dress up when there won't be any tourists to see you."

"Perhaps, but this keeps me in the spirit of my role. I can practice greeting important people with the grace and charm of a southern belle."

Jennifer fastened the last hook. "Don't you think you're carrying this a little far?"

Her mother spun around and flipped open a fan suspended from her wrist by a silken cord. "Of course not, darling," she drawled as she fluttered the dark blue silk and ivory fan beside her face. "I'm simply enjoying my job. Wait until you see my performance on Founder's Day. This year, for the first time ever, we are staging a stunning re-enactment of Henrietta Dutton's charge up Dutton Heights. I get goose bumps just thinking about it."

Snapping shut her accessory, Mary lifted her skirts with both hands and headed for the door. "I won't be back until late, so don't wait up. Thank goodness I don't have to wear a hoop under this thing. I'd never be able to drive in it. But I do wish I had a carriage to ride in. It would so much more appropriate to arrive in a horse-drawn buggy than in my truck."

As her mother departed in a flurry of petti-coats, Jennifer glanced to where her brothers and sister sat on the sofa. They were all watching her with various degrees of concern on their faces.

Lizzie said, "It's tough enough being the brainy girl in school. Having a mother who thinks she is Betsy Ross on top of that is the pits."

"Mom does get a bit carried away," Jennifer admitted.

Toby rose and brought his empty plate to the sink. "Carried away? Our mother is a nut case. She knows more about old Colonel Dutton and his weirdo wife than they did. Who cares what was happening in 1859, anyway?"

Their mother's passion for re-enacting the past sometimes seemed to border on an obsession, but Jennifer felt the need to defend her.

"If it wasn't for Mom's respect for the history of our town and her determination to save our heritage, Henrietta Dutton's deeds of valor would be forgotten."

"And the town council wouldn't have an excuse to hold a money-making festival every year and exploit mother's zeal, not to mention her time and energy," Lizzie added.

"When did you get to be such a cynic?" Jennifer asked.

"Between your job and school and riding, I'm the only one left to listen to her grand schemes to expand the widow Dutton's ride into a national event."

"I'm here," Toby said, elbowing his sister when he sat down beside her.

Lizzie elbowed him back. "Oh, like you listen to her. All she talks about is making the exact same ride to show the world how brave Henrietta Dutton was. Mom doesn't even ask about school or how my chess match went."

"How did your match go?" Jennifer asked, feeling guilty for not asking sooner.

"I won—as usual. Most boys only think they're smarter."

Her comment started another round of elbowing with Toby. Ryan moved to the floor to get away from his jousting siblings.

"Cut it out," Jennifer said sternly. "I'm sure things will get back to normal after the Founder's Day Festival. Making the past come alive is Mother's dream. We need to support her."

Jennifer opened her textbook and prayed that she was right, but she couldn't quite silence the nagging doubts at the back of her mind. The kids needed a mother who was involved in their lives, not one so involved with the past that she couldn't see the present. How did one tell their own parent that they were falling down on their job?

The Founder's Day Festival was only three weeks away. Jennifer would hold her peace until then, but after her mother made her big ride, they were going to have a mother-daughter heart-to-heart.

* * *

On Monday afternoon, when Jennifer was done with her classes for the day, she made her way through the veterinary hospital wards and down the short hall to the front desk at the Large Animal Clinic.

Her mother's behavior was still on her mind, but she wasn't as worried as she had been the day before. The entire family had spent Sunday together in a normal, modern-day fashion. They had attended church together and spent the afternoon visiting friends of the family. By the end of the day Jennifer decided that she had been making mountains out of mole hills.

Stephanie, another student who worked part-time in the clinic, sighed with relief when Jennifer opened the office door. "Am I glad to see you."

"Busy day?" Jennifer tucked her purse into the gray metal cabinet beside the desk and took a chair behind the glass partition that separated them from the client waiting area.

"Three emergency surgeries on cows, two bad lacerations on a pair of draft horses and a sonogram to check if a llama is pregnant. Nothing too weird. I just need to get going. I've got an anatomy test this afternoon and I really have to study."

"Is there anything I need to know?"

"Dr. Wilkes just brought in a ton of stuff to be filed." Stephanie transferred a large stack of papers to Jennifer's side of the desk.

"Oh, joy." Dr. Wilkes was notorious for his bad penmanship.

Stephanie bit her lower lip. "Do you want me to stay and help?"

"No, I've got it. Go cram to your heart's content."

"You're a doll, Jennifer."

"Yes, I know," Jennifer said, nodding sagely.

Stephanie giggled, then hurried out the door. Jennifer picked up an armful of papers and carried them to the shoulder-high black filing cabinets lining the wall behind her. She peered closely at Dr. Wilkes illegible scrawl and tried to decide if the first letter of the client's last name was an A, an O or a misshapen D.

Fifteen files later, her eyes were beginning to cross when the sound of the front door opening made her look up in relief. Anything was better than this.

To her surprise, Edmond Barnes walked in followed by his chauffeur. His driver held a glass bowl overflowing with a bright bouquet of autumn-colored flowers.

She smiled at Avery's grandfather, happy to

see he was looking much better. "Mr. Barnes, what are you doing here?"

He took the bouquet from his driver. "I've brought a small gift to repay your kindness the other day, Miss Grant."

"You didn't have to do that." Jennifer looked at the small opening in the glass partition between them, then hurried out of the office door and around to the waiting area.

He extended the flowers to her. "I didn't have to do it, I wanted to do it."

"How on earth did you know that I worked here?"

"You said you were a veterinary student. A few phone calls was all it took to discover that you both attend school and are employed here."

Taken aback, she said, "That's actually a little scary."

His expression showed his surprise followed quickly by genuine distress. "I'm very sorry, Miss Grant. The last thing I want to do is upset you. Please enjoy the flowers and the knowledge that your kindness touched me deeply."

"I will, thank you very much." She couldn't contain her curiosity any longer. Although it was clearly none of her business, she couldn't help wondering if Mr. Barnes and Avery had made any progress in repairing their relationship.

"Have you been able to accomplish what you came here for?" she asked, hoping he and Avery had been able to heal their breach.

"Reconciling with my grandson? I'm sorry to say I have not, but I'm taking your advice. I don't plan to give up on him. I did that once and it was my biggest mistake. I'll be staying in the area for a while, although the service at my current motel leaves a lot to be desired."

"That's an easy fix." Turning around, she retraced her steps into the office. Setting the flowers on the desk, she pulled her purse from the cabinet and withdrew a card for the bed and breakfast next to the café where her mother worked. She slipped it under the glass toward him.

"This place is on the main street of my hometown. It's only a few miles from here on Highway 24. It's called the Dutton Inn, but it's a bed and breakfast. The owners, Mr. and Mrs. Marcus, belong to our church so I can vouch for them. It's quiet, immaculately clean and the beds have real feather mattresses."

Edmond took the card. "That certainly sounds better than where I've been staying."

"I'm sure you'll like it. The town has a historical section that you may enjoy exploring. If you want a really knowledgeable tour guide, my mother, Mary Grant, works at the café next door. She'll be happy to bend your ear about our history."

"I may do that. Thank you once again for your kindness and consideration."

Just then the outside door opened again. Captain Watson and Avery walked in.

Jennifer pressed her lips together and looked down. How long would it take until the sight of Avery's face stopped twisting her heart with yearning?

Calling herself every kind of fool, she pasted a polite smile on her face and greeted them. "Good afternoon, gentlemen. How may I help you?"

Avery stopped in shock at the sight of his grandfather talking to Jennifer. He had assumed, wrongly it seemed, that the old man had gone back to Boston.

Hanging back as Captain Watson approached the desk and asked to speak with Dr. Cutter, Avery tried to figure out why the head of his family's empire was still in Kansas.

What motive could Edmond have for remaining in the area? Something wasn't right.

His grandfather didn't trust the day-to-day running of his company to anyone. In all the years Avery had known him, he could only remember him missing work once. The day of his son and daughter-in-law's funeral. The next day, he had gone back to his office, leaving Avery alone in the sprawling mansion.

Jennifer picked up the phone and spoke to Dr. Cutter, then hung up and said, "You may go in, Captain."

Avery spoke up quickly. "If you don't need me, sir, I'll wait here."

Captain Watson glanced at Avery sharply, but nodded. "I think I can handle it. I shouldn't be long."

When his captain left, Avery gave his full attention to his grandfather. "I don't know how you knew I would be here today, but I don't have anything to say to you."

Edmond gave him a tight smile. "I'm sorry you feel that way. I simply stopped by to thank Miss Grant for her kindness the other day. I had no idea you would be here."

Avery wasn't sure if he should believe him or not.

With a slight bow, Edmond said, "You have my phone number if you decide you wish to speak with me. Until then, I bid you good day."

He walked past Avery and left the clinic followed closely by his burley and stoic driver.

Avery watched his grandfather leave, but he

knew it wasn't going to be easy to dismiss the man from his thoughts. Curiosity had the better of him now. What did Edmond have to gain by staying in town?

For a moment, Avery considered the possibility that his grandfather might actually want a reconciliation. The second the idea popped into his head, Avery dismissed it as foolish. And so was the notion that Jennifer had somehow arranged it. His grandfather never allowed sentimentality to influence his decisions.

"He seems like a nice man." Jennifer said, drawing Avery away from his speculations.

"He isn't."

She looked down. "People change sometimes."

"Not very often."

He stepped up to the glass in front of the desk. Jennifer turned away and began filing papers, allowing him to spend a few moments admiring her feminine curves.

Watching her, he began to consider that he may have lost more than he'd gained when he'd broken it off with her. He'd been angry when he learned Jennifer had gone behind his back to contact Edmond.

Avery didn't want anyone to know what a fool he'd made of himself over a scheming woman. Jennifer had made a mistake, but at least *her* intentions had been good. At the time, her tearful apology and explanation had fallen on deaf ears. All he saw was one more woman who'd betrayed his trust.

He didn't trust easily, but he'd trusted Jennifer more than anyone in a long time. That was what hurt the most. His attempts at revenge hadn't eased his pain. They only managed to make him feel worse.

But he felt better now that he was near her.

I miss her. I miss the way she used to smile at me.

Giving himself a mental shake, he looked down. It didn't matter what he missed. Anything they might have shared between them was long gone. His behavior had made sure of that.

"How have you been?" he asked when the silence had stretched on long enough.

"Fine, thank you."

"That's good. How did your meet go last Saturday?"

"Fine, thank you." Her tone didn't vary.

"I guess that means you won again. Lee says you're one of the best riders in the state."

"Lee is too kind."

"He's a fan of yours, for sure. How is it that I didn't know you were so accomplished? You never went to any shows when we were going out."

"We went out during the winter. The shows run from April through November."

"That makes sense. It's the same for our unit's exhibitions. To become such an expert you must have had a good teacher." His show of interest sounded lame even to his own ears.

"I did." She opened another file drawer without looking at him.

"Who taught you?"

She slammed the file drawer closed and turned to face him. "What do you want?"

He spread his hands wide. "I'm just making conversation."

"I don't think so."

"All right, I'm interested in learning the same type of fancy riding that you do. Who taught you?"

"My grandmother was my coach."

He decided to cut to the chase. "Does she give lessons?"

"She passed away two years ago."

"I'm sorry to hear that." So much for his plan to take lessons from the person who had trained her.

"Thank you. I miss her very much. Perhaps that's why I tried to intervene with you and your grandfather. I know how final it is when you lose them and how much you wish you had had more time with them."

"I've had more than enough time with Edmond. Look, I need to find someone to teach me the basic dressage moves in the next couple of weeks. Money is not an object. I'll double the going price for lessons. Are you interested?"

She tossed the papers she held onto her desk and folded her arms across her middle. "You're joking, right?"

"I'm rarely serious, but today is the exception to the rule."

"Why?"

"What does that matter?"

She tilted her head. "Humor me."

"Have you heard of the American Cavalry Competition?"

"Of course. I've watched it several times."

"It's going to be held at Fort Riley next month and I plan to compete for the Sheridan Cup."

"I remember now. There's a military dressage class, isn't there?"

"It counts for one quarter of the overall score. The saber class is a lock for me and I'm sure I can finish in the top three with a pistol, but Lee tells me I need a dressage coach and I believe him. He's seen some of the other riders in action. So, what do you say?"

"No."

"What? I just offered you twice the going rate for a few measly lessons."

"And I said no. I don't care what you offer to pay me. Money is not an object."

His temper flared at being thwarted. "You're just afraid you won't be able to keep your hands off me."

Her eyes narrowed. "That is so true. I can picture them around your scrawny neck right this minute."

"That's not a very Christian attitude, Jenny," he chided.

Her eyebrows shot up. She opened her mouth and closed it again without saying anything.

He knew a moment's satisfaction at seeing her speechless, but it quickly evaporated when he watched her bite her lower lip. He had kissed those full sweet lips before. He wanted to kiss her again.

She said, "It wasn't a very Christian thing to say, but as you so clearly pointed out to me when we were dating, you are not a Christian. Good luck in finding someone to give you lessons." She picked up her papers and turned her back on him.

The captain came out of Dr. Cutter's office with a smile on his face. "Good news. Dr. Cutter has cleared Dakota to return to full duty. I can't wait to tell the rest of the men. With proper conditioning, he should be fit to ride in the competition."

"That is good news, sir." Avery glanced toward Jennifer.

She still stood with her back to him. Once upon a time her face would have beamed with delight at such news. She, as much as anyone, had worked to save Dakota and return him to a full and active life. He wanted her to be happy. He wanted her to smile.

As the captain left the building, Avery hung back. Before he could lose his nerve, he rapped sharply on the glass. Startled by the sound, she spun around.

He shoved his hands in his pockets. "I just wanted to say that I know I treated you badly and I'm sorry."

Jennifer clutched the papers she was holding tightly to her chest. An apology from Avery was the last thing she expected. If Isabella had hopped in and asked for a carrot in perfect English, Jennifer might have been more stunned, but not by much.

She waited without speaking. Somehow, he

was going to turn it into a jest or an insult, she just knew it.

Only he didn't. For a second, she thought she saw sadness cloud his eyes.

He shrugged and gave her a little smile. "Guess I'll see you around."

With that, he turned and walked out, leaving the bell over the door tinkling merrily and the faintest scent of his cologne wafting through the opening in the partition.

Jennifer stared after him in amazement. The man had actually apologized. She wouldn't have believed it if she hadn't heard it with her own ears.

Perhaps he wasn't such a lost cause after all.

Not that she cared anymore. Reaching out she touched the soft petal of a yellow lily in the bouquet his grandfather had left.

"Who am I kidding?" she whispered. "I do care. Oh, so much more than I should."

Chapter Five

Jennifer realized she was still clutching her files and laid them on the counter. The more she thought about it, the odder Avery's comment seemed.

"Wow! He actually apologized to me. I'm going to have to mark this day on my calendar." She repeated his comment with emphasis and wished she had thought of it before he left.

She couldn't allow herself to be taken in by the man again. She had more backbone than that.

But he *had* sounded sincere. She could almost believe that he meant it.

No, it was way out of character for him. Was he trying to butter her up and get her to change her mind about becoming his riding coach?

"Right. Like that will happen."

She had too much sense to get involved with

him again, even if some small part of her still found him attractive. "Once burned is twice shy, as my grandma used to say."

Brian walked into the office with Isabella in her carrier and a cardboard box balanced on top of it. He deposited his burden on the counter. "Who are you talking to?"

She pulled herself together. "No one. Are you leaving now?"

"I am. Thanks for watching Isabella for us."

"Don't mention it. Where are you and Lindsey off to?"

"We're off to Houston. Do you remember Corporal Shane Ross?"

"The tall Texan from the color guard? Sure."

"He and his wife just had a little girl. He's stationed in Germany, but he's here in the States on a short leave. Annie, his wife, will be joining him overseas when she and the baby get cleared to travel. Since Shane will have to go back before then, Lindsey is going to be staying with Annie for the next few weeks."

"Be sure and tell him that I said hello."

"I will. Any questions about Isabella's care?"

She smiled and shook her head. "None."

"If you need me for anything, you can always get me on my cell phone."

"Don't worry about a thing."

"Remember that Isabella likes to chew on pencils when she is bored, so you should make sure she gets plenty of attention."

"My littlest brother is looking forward to playing with her again, so I don't think that will be a problem."

"I put several of her favorite toys in the box with her food and litter. I'm sure you know not to give her iceberg lettuce, but a romaine is okay."

Jennifer rose and moved to hold open the office door for Brian. "Isabella will be fine."

"Of course she will."

He started to leave, but stopped and turned to her. "Don't forget that she also chews on any paper she can get hold of."

"Oh, good. I'll use that excuse if I can't get my statistic paper done on time. 'I'm sorry, Professor Carlton, Dr. Cutter's rabbit ate my homework.'"

"You wouldn't."

"I'm kidding." She gave him a gentle push out the door.

"Are you sure you don't have any questions?"

"I'm sure. She'll be fine. Will you?"

He relaxed and grinned at her. "I think so. I just hate leaving her."

"No? I never would have guessed."

"Okay, I'm going." He made it as far as the

clinic door before he stopped again. "I almost forgot. Dr. Wilkes is covering my calls while I'm gone. Be nice to him."

Jennifer waved as Brian walked out the door. When he was gone at last, she returned to her chair and sat down to gaze at Isabella. "Oh, joy, more illegible charts to decipher. What did I do to deserve this? No, don't answer that. I've had enough shocks for one day."

Putting Isabella's cage on the office floor, Jennifer returned to the filing waiting for her and tried to avoid thinking about Avery. It was a losing battle. When six o'clock rolled around at last, she happily turned the office over to the senior vet student who had the night watch and locked the clinic doors.

It wasn't until she pulled into her own driveway and saw her littlest brother come dashing out of the house that she was finally able to banish a certain soldier's puzzling behavior from her mind.

Ryan barely waited until the truck came to a stop before he pulled open her door. "Did you bring her? Did you?"

"I did." Jennifer lifted the carrier from the seat beside her and handed it to him.

He peered into the cage. "Hi, Isabella. Remember me?"

Jennifer smiled indulgently. "I'm sure she does."

"I've got a place for you to sleep all fixed up in my room," he cooed to the rabbit. He looked up at Jennifer with a wide beaming grin.

It was the happiest she had seen him in months. She didn't have the heart to tell him that Isabella had to sleep in her cage. That bit of news could wait until bedtime.

Jennifer glanced toward the spot where her mother usually parked. There was no sign of her truck. The horse trailer was gone, too. "Isn't Mom here?"

"Nope." He jumped down with Isabella's cage and started toward the front door.

"Did she call and say she would be late?" Jennifer asked as she stepped out of her vehicle and pulled Isabella's stuff out from behind her seat. Their mother was almost always home before the kids got out of school. It was one of the reasons she worked the early shift at the café.

"Don't know." Ryan disappeared into the house with the rabbit leaving Jennifer to wonder why her mother wasn't back yet. Surely she didn't have another festival planning meeting.

Following her brother inside, Jennifer saw Toby and Lizzie crowding around Ryan as he lifted Isabella out of her carrier. Watching all three of them stroking Brian's pet, Jennifer knew he needn't have worried that she wouldn't get enough attention.

"Lizzie, did Mom call?" Jennifer asked, setting her box on the pink and white Formica kitchen counter.

Shaking her head, Lizzie said, "She didn't call here."

"That's odd." Jennifer could plainly see there weren't any messages on the answering machine on the counter beside her box.

Toby looked up. "What's for supper? I'm starving."

Lizzie rolled her eyes. "You're always hungry."

"Are the chores done?" Jennifer asked quickly, hoping to forestall an argument between the two.

Ryan piped up. "I took the trash out."

The deafening silence from the others told Jennifer what she already suspected. She pointed toward the door. With a last, quick pat for the rabbit, Lizzie and Toby went out to feed and care for the other animals with only minor grumbling.

Jennifer picked up the phone and dialed her mother's cell phone, but it went straight to voicemail. Staff members at Old Towne weren't permitted to carry cell phones during business hours, but Mary always turned hers on once she left work.

After leaving a brief message, Jennifer hung up and set about finding something to make into a quick meal. Thirty minutes later, Jennifer was dishing out helpings of spaghetti when she heard the sound of her mother's truck pulling in. Her relief mingled with a growing sense of annoyance. She could only hope her mother had a good explanation as to why she hadn't called.

Toby and Lizzie were already seated at the table, but Ryan was still on the floor rolling a red plastic ball for Isabella to chase. At the sound of the truck door slamming, he jumped up and raced toward the entryway. "Mom's home."

Jennifer dropped the pan on the table and made a dive for the rabbit. She caught her just as Ryan threw open the door.

Mary rushed in, still wearing her calico work dress. "I'm sorry I'm late. We had a last-minute meeting with Mayor Jenks. You won't believe what he wants us to do now."

Ryan bounced up and down beside her. "Mom, Mom, Mom, Jennifer brought Isabella home with her. It's okay if she sleeps in my bed, isn't it?" he begged.

Mary's eyes widened as she caught sight of

the rabbit squirming in Jennifer's grasp and she snatched up the front of her skirt with both hands. "Do not put that beast on the floor. She ruined two of my best petticoats the last time she was here."

"I've got her," Jennifer reassured her mother.

Later, Jennifer could never be sure if it was the sight of so much white lace or the sound of her mother scrunching up her crinoline that set the rabbit off. Whatever it was, the usually docile bunny suddenly leapt out of Jennifer's grasp and dashed beneath Mary's skirt.

Shrieking, Mary spun around, flapping the fabric of her dress as she attempted to escape Isabella's excited leaps.

Jennifer dropped to her knees and tried to catch the culprit, but Isabella darted underneath her mother's petticoats. Lizzie and Tony began howling with laughter.

Ryan yelled, "Don't step on her!" and threw himself under her skirt to save his friend.

Jennifer saw the fall coming but was powerless to prevent it. Her mother went down in a flurry of white lace and crinoline.

Ryan emerged with Isabella in his arms. Lizzie, Toby and Jennifer all rushed to help their mother up. Clearly shaken, Mary tried to rise, but sank back with a loud moan of pain.

* * *

Four hours later, Jennifer sat in the hospital emergency waiting area and listened as the doctor detailed her mother's injury.

"Mrs. Grant has a badly sprained wrist and the MRI shows that she has a severely torn ligament in her right knee."

Jennifer's heart sank. "Will she need surgery?"

"We can try keeping it immobilized, but I think chances are slim that it will heal without surgery. Either way, she is going to need a few months of rehabilitation."

"A few months?"

"I wish the news were better."

"Thank you, Doctor. You've been very kind."

"You're quite welcome. I must say, tonight was a first for me."

"How so?"

"I've never been called on to treat a patient in a Victorian ball gown who claims she tripped over a rabbit."

Jennifer managed a wry smile. "It's a Victorian day dress, actually, but I can see how you might not be up on 1850s fashions. If you knew my family, you would know that this is really nothing too strange for us. Can I see her now?"

"Certainly. We've given her something for the pain and we're getting a splint and crutches for her. She can go home tonight, but she needs to see an orthopedic specialist as soon as possible. This is his number."

Jennifer took the information the doctor handed her along with her mother's discharge instructions and then followed him to the small curtained cubical. Her mother lay propped up on a narrow cart.

"Hey, Mom. How are you doing?"

It was obvious that Mary had been crying. "I'm going to miss my Founder's Day ride. I worked so hard for that."

"I'm sorry, Mom. This is all my fault. I honestly intended to keep the rabbit in my room and not let her out when you were home. I just got sidetracked and forgot that Ryan had her out of her cage."

Mary nodded and reached out to pat her daughter's arm. "I know you didn't mean any harm, dear. I just don't know how I'm going to tell the Festival committee. We have all put so much time and effort into re-enacting Henrietta Dutton's ride. I can't let everyone down this way."

Jennifer was a lot more worried about how she was going to pay the hospital bill. They did have a little insurance, but the deductible was five-thousand dollars. Money already earmarked for Jennifer's school fees. If her mother needed surgery it would mean withdrawing from school until next year.

"You didn't let anyone down, Mom. You have a torn ligament in your knee. It's not like you decided to take a trip to the mall, instead."

"You don't understand. Announcements have been sent to newspapers and historical associations all across the country. We have descendants of the Dutton family coming from as far away as New York and Tennessee for this. We simply can't cancel now."

"Maybe someone else from the committee can take your place."

"I don't know who. Certain not Edna Marcus, even if she is a great-great-great-niece of the woman. She couldn't fit into one of Henrietta's gowns if she stayed on bread and water until doomsday. You're going to have to take my place, Jennifer. I don't see any other way."

"Me?" Her voice actually squeaked.

Mary nodded. "You and I are the same size. We won't have to alter the costume. You're a better rider than I am. You won't have any trouble making the charge up Dutton Heights."

Jennifer shook her head. "I don't think so."

"Please. You know how much this means to me."

Jennifer did know. And it was her fault that

her mother wouldn't be able to fulfill the dream she had worked so hard to make come true.

"I suppose I could wear the dress for one afternoon and ride up a hill, but I draw the line at wearing a corset."

Mary scowled and tried to sit up, but winced in pain. Holding her bandaged wrist close, she said sternly, "This is a historical re-enactment, Jennifer. We are striving for the utmost accuracy. The costume must be exact."

"And exactly what does that mean?"

"As was the custom of the day, Henrietta was wearing a corset, pantaloon and three petticoats beneath her simple cotton dress when she pulled a saber from her dead husband's hand, threw herself on his war horse and led a band of ordinary farmers in a battle-turning charge straight up Dutton Heights into the very teeth of a pack of murderous raiders."

Jennifer sighed in resignation. Who could argue with that type of fanatical logic? This was a lose-lose situation. "Okay, okay, I'll do it."

"You will? Oh, darling, you have no idea how happy that makes me." Mary sniffed and used the corner of the sheet to blot her eyes.

When she regained her composure, she said, "You'll have to start practicing right away."

"Practice what? I thought I was just going to ride up a hill in a dress."

"Oh, no. You must do exactly what Henrietta did."

"Mom, she rode up a hill."

Mary shook her head. "Haven't you been listening? She picked up her husband's saber and his pistol and rode straight into the enemy camp. She struck down six of the brigands with her saber and shot two more with her husband's pistol before jumping her horse over the wall where their leader cowered and demanded his surrender at the point of her sword."

"She did all that?"

"Eye witnesses attest to the fact. The Lord was truly at her side."

"He must have been. So I have to wave a sword while I ride up this hill?"

"Not wave it. You'll have to cut down six bandits and shoot two more. Of course, they'll simply be mannequins dressed to look like fearsome raiders. They are rigged to fall down when you strike them or shoot them. It isn't as easy as it sounds. I've been practicing for six months and I'm not perfect yet."

"Mom, do you own a saber and a pistol?" Jennifer didn't try to hide her astonishment

"Of course, dear. I store them at the Dutton

house in a trunk for safe keeping. I wouldn't want the boys playing with them. Someone might get hurt."

Mary bit her lip as her brows drew together in a frown. "With less than three weeks until the festival, you're going to need a professional coach to master using a saber and pistol from horseback. I certainly won't be a position to teach you."

"How on earth did you learn?" Jennifer couldn't imagine her mother galloping across the countryside wielding a sword or shooting a gun.

"Gerard taught me."

Jennifer racked her brain, but could only come up with one Gerard. Surely her mother didn't mean the short, bald man who worked at the local supermarket. "Gerard Hoover from the produce section at the grocery store?"

"Yes. He's a cavalry re-enactor with a Civil War unit. I know he would be happy to help but his unit is in South Carolina for a re-enactment and he wouldn't be back until a few days before the festival. He's playing Colonel Dutton for us. You have friends in the mounted color guard at Fort Riley. Perhaps one of them could show you the basics."

Avery's face flashed into Jennifer's mind.

She saw his self-assured smile and that gleam in his eyes.

No, there was simply no way she was going to ask him.

Chapter Six

Avery pulled his apartment door open and stared in stunned surprise at the sight of Jennifer Grant on his doorstep, one hand raised to knock again. She took a startled step backward, her hand going to catch the strap of her purse as it slipped from her shoulder.

She was wearing a blue, short-sleeved sweater over a pair of black jeans. Her hair was loose about her face and the afternoon sun highlighted the honey-colored strands.

A thrill of happiness shot through him at the sight of her. He quickly struggled to suppress the emotion. "Well, well, well. What do we have here?"

She raised her hand again, palm out. "Stop. Don't say anything that will make me regret coming here more than I already do."

Folding his arms over his chest, he waited, wondering what had prompted this visit. Could his grandfather have put her up to it? He wouldn't put it past him.

Lowering her hand, she took a deep breath. "Do you still want a riding coach?"

"Maybe."

"If I agree to give you lessons, I need something in return."

"I've already offered to pay you."

"I don't need the money. Well, I do need the money, but I need something else more than I need the money—which I can't believe I just said—but that's why I've come to you."

"I'm almost afraid to ask what you're talking about."

She shifted from one foot to the other. "I need to learn how to use a sword."

He raised an eyebrow. "I'll bite. Why?"

"It's a long story." She brushed past him and walked into his apartment.

As he started to close the door, he noticed the black SUV parked down the block across the street from his complex. It looked like the same one he had seen several times in the past few days, once behind him when he left the fort and once again outside the restaurant where he had dinner. Shrugging off the sensation of being watched, Avery closed the door and followed Jennifer.

In his living room, she dropped onto one of the brown leather chairs that faced his matching sofa across a glass-topped oak coffee table.

"Can I get you something to drink?" he offered. "A soda, some tea?"

"Thank you, but I can't stay long. I have class in half an hour so I'll get right to the point. My mother was recently injured in an accident and she won't be able to ride for several months. I'm taking her place in an authentic re-creation of Henrietta Dutton's charge up Dutton Heights for the Founder's Day Festival."

"In Dutton. Sure I know about it. Our unit will be carrying the colors for the opening ceremony."

"Good. Anyway, to take my mother's place I have to be able to strike down six targets with a saber and shoot two more with a pistol while riding at a full gallop. Can you teach me to do that?"

"Sure."

"In two weeks time?" She looked skeptical.

"Maybe. Why ask me?"

She hesitated, then said, "My mother's instructor is unavailable. I called your captain to ask about getting lessons from your unit's saber instructor."

"Which is me."

"Yes, I was informed that you had taken over the position after Corporal Ross left."

"I told you I was the best, but I'm sure Lee would be happy to teach you what he knows."

"Believe me, I thought about asking him, but I wouldn't be able to pay him for his time."

"He'd do it for nothing."

She looked down at her hands clasped together in her lap. "Perhaps, but I wouldn't feel right about accepting his charity."

"But you're okay with accepting charity from me?"

Her gaze locked with his. "You and I are bartering one skill for another. I teach you and you teach me. No charity involved, no strings attached."

He walked into the small kitchen, opened the refrigerator door and pulled out a bottle of water. He took a drink, then tossed the cap into the trash. Leaning back against the counter, he said, "I'll have to think it over."

Jennifer wanted to wipe the smug look off his face but forced herself to stay calm. For some reason, the good Lord had seen fit to test her with this burden. She wouldn't turn away from it, so she swallowed her pride because her mother was depending on her.

Relaxing her fingers, she rubbed her palms on her pants legs. "If you're worried that our past relationship will get in the way, I can assure you it won't."

"How can I be sure? This might just be a ploy to get back into my good graces."

"You don't have good graces. You have an ego the size of an elephant."

"Insulting the man you want to help you isn't a move I would have made."

She clenched her hands into fists. She hated to admit that he was right.

Forcing a smile to her lips, she said, "I have no interest in renewing our personal relationship. We gave it a shot and we turned out to be wrong for each other. If we leave it at that, I don't see why we can't provide each other with a mutually beneficial service. I know you want to win the Sheridan Cup. I want to keep my mother's commitment. We can work together to make this happen or we can fail separately. It's up to you."

"No strings attached?"

"None."

"No religion shoved in my face?"

Her eyes narrowed. "I will not pretend that my faith isn't an important part of my life."

"If I say yes, what's your plan?"

She relaxed. "My plan is to meet at my house in the afternoons for the next two weeks. We have an outdoor arena. Which horse will you be riding?"

"Does it matter?"

"Yes, it does."

"I plan to ride Dakota."

She nodded. "I know Dakota has had formal training. Lindsey told me her brother used to show him before he gave the horse to your unit. Is he in good enough condition for the jumping part of it?"

"I think he is. He's fast and he loves to jump."

She looked hopeful for the first time. "Then you'll do it?"

"As long as you keep your end of the bargain and this stays strictly business, I don't see that I have anything to lose."

"Good. I'll see you tomorrow at four."

"Make it four-thirty. Shall I bring Dakota?"

"No. You should ride my McCloud. Riding a well-trained horse is one way to learn how it should be done, but bring your own saddle."

Jennifer couldn't believe he had agreed to her proposal so easily. While she was relieved, some small part of her couldn't help but wonder why. Another nagging little voice told her keeping things professional might prove difficult.

Avery drove down the road leading to Jennifer's home at the appointed time the next afternoon. As he approached the double wide mobile home, he couldn't help but compare it to the house he had grown up in. The entire trailer would have fit into the garage that had housed his father's sports cars or into the boathouse where his grandfather's sailboats were moored.

He spotted two boys on a tire swing suspended from the branches of a gnarled oak tree inside the fenced yard.

They must be Jennifer's brothers. Even though he and Jennifer had dated for several months, he had successfully avoided meeting most of her family. He'd been introduced to her younger sister when Jennifer brought her to one of the CGMCG performances. The rest of the time, he managed to pick Jennifer up when she got out of class or right after she got off work.

Meeting family implied commitment—something he avoided like the plague. So why had he agreed to come here today?

Avery had been trying to find the answer to that question ever since Jennifer showed up at his apartment. He wasn't used to studying his own motives but he recognized that guilt was playing an unexpected role.

Of course, he would benefit from their arrangement, too. He couldn't forget that winning the Sheridan Cup was his goal. Spending time with Jennifer would simply be icing on the cake.

As he pulled to a stop, Avery noticed the taller boy turning the tire around and around with the smaller, blond boy sitting inside it. Both of them were dressed in worn jeans and long-sleeved western chambray shirts. The little one's shirt had a patch on one elbow and was baggy enough to make Avery suspect it had been a hand-me-down from his brother.

Avery climbed out of his car just as the older boy finished twisting the rope. He gave the tire a hearty shove and stepped back, letting his brother spin through space with wild squeals of laughter filling the air.

It looked like fun. Until Avery had joined the army he had led a life of privilege few people knew, but the cars, boats and the servants working silently in the cavernous house hadn't supplied a lonely boy with a chance to engage in the kind of amusement he witnessed now. The envy he felt startled him.

When the tire finally stopped spinning, the

older boy realized they were being watched. He left the swing and glared at Avery over the fence. His younger sibling tried to follow, but ended up staggering back and forth, then abruptly sat on the ground.

The door of the trailer opened and Jennifer came down the steps wearing blue jeans and a pink jean jacket over a white T-shirt. Her pants were tucked into black riding boots. She looked eager to get to work. He could almost imagine she was happy to see him. He closed the car door and leaned against it as he waited for her.

She stopped a few feet away and slipped her hands in the front pockets of her jeans. "Hi."

Her hair was drawn back into a ponytail, but wisps of it danced free at her temples. They tempted him to smooth them down with his hand, to cup the soft skin of her cheek with his palm and draw his thumb across the fullness of her lips.

He folded his arms across his chest to keep from reaching for her and hardened his resolve against the desire.

There was no sense torturing himself. She'd made it clear she wasn't looking to rekindle their relationship. She needed his help and he needed hers. This was business. He had a trophy to win. She was his ticket to the winner's circle.

"So, who gets their lesson first?" Avery

asked. It wasn't hard to sound bored. He'd had plenty of practice. He knew how to keep a tight rein on his emotions.

Some of the eagerness left her eyes, but she made a quick recovery and lifted her chin. "Since I have two weeks to get ready and you have three weeks until your competition, I think it only fair that we start with me. I have my mother's horse saddled down at the barn. We can get started now if you're ready."

"No horse just yet." When Jennifer scowled at him, he smiled. "The first saber lesson takes place on the ground."

He turned and opened his car door, then pulled out a wooden broomstick and offered it to her.

She cocked one eyebrow. "What's this?"

"Your saber, madame."

The older boy snickered. The little one, who had gained his feet and was standing at the fence, tried his best to stifle his own chuckles with both hands clasped over his mouth.

Jennifer sent them both a quelling stare. "Avery, these are my brothers, Ryan and Toby. Pay no attention to them."

"I'm Ryan," the little one said eagerly. His older brother didn't say anything, but the expression on his face made it clear that he already disliked his sister's tutor.

Jennifer looked at Avery and then down at the stick he held out to her. "You're kidding, right?"

"Not at all."

"What can I learn with this?"

"How not to cut off your foot or slice your horse's neck. Let's see what you've got." He tossed the wooden dowel to her.

She deftly caught it in the middle. With a quick flick of her wrist, she began twirling it like a baton, spinning it from one hand to the next until it was a whirling blur.

After a few seconds, she tossed the stick into the air, spun around once, caught it neatly by one end and tapped the other end on the ground. Then, tucking the rod beneath one arm, she raised her hand with a flourish. Grinning widely, she said, "That's what I've got. What do you have?"

He snatched it from her grasp. "A long two weeks ahead of me."

She wrinkled her nose. "You're not the only one."

He glared at her and she glared back. Finally, he asked, "Do you want to learn this or not? Because I can leave."

The sound of the door opening caused them both to glance toward the trailer. Jennifer's mother hobbled awkwardly out the front door using one crutch. A long black brace encased her right leg and a blue sling held her right arm close to her body. She carried a bundle of yellow cloth draped across one shoulder. A teenage girl with dark curls followed her out of the house.

Jennifer rushed toward them. "Mother, don't you dare try to get down those steps."

"I'm not. Stop fussing." Grimacing with pain, Mrs. Grant propped herself against the wooden porch railing. She pulled the fabric from her shoulder and held it out to Jennifer. "You're going to need this."

"What is it?"

"One of my skirts. It just ties at the waist. You can slip it on over what you're wearing now."

"I don't need this, yet."

"You'll have to accustom yourself to moving in full skirts and petticoats. It takes practice and you don't have much time. Aren't you going to introduce me to your friend?"

Avery saw Jennifer's hesitation. He stepped forward as she said, "Mom, this is Avery Barnes. Avery, this is my mother, Mary Grant."

"It's nice to meet you at last, Mr. Barnes. Jennifer has spoken of you often."

"Nothing good," Lizzie muttered, folding her arms across her chest.

"I'm sure," he said with a self-conscious

smile. He easily read the wariness on the faces of Jennifer's family.

Mary spoke to her youngest daughter. "Lizzie, don't be rude." Looking at Jennifer, she said, "I'm sure you have lots of work to do so we won't keep you."

"You need to be resting that leg," Jennifer scolded, climbing the steps to hold open the door.

"I'm tired of sitting on the sofa."

"I don't care. The doctor won't start therapy until some of the swelling goes down and it won't go down until you stay off your feet. Lizzie, sit on her if you have to to keep her down."

Mary said, "I'll go back to the sofa when you put this skirt on."

"I'll put it on after you're safely on the couch with that leg on a pillow," Jennifer countered.

"She's quite bossy, Mr. Barnes." Mary said, maneuvering herself to head inside.

"I've noticed that about her," he agreed. Oddly, he also liked that about her.

Jennifer vanished into the house with her mother and sister, leaving Avery alone with her brothers. Toby glanced toward the house then back at Avery. He stepped closer to the fence with a fierce scowl on his face. "If you make my sister cry again I'm going to knock your block off."

"Yeah! That goes for me, too." Ryan added, imitating his brother's defensive stance.

Toby spun on his heels and stalked off. Avery watched him leave, then glanced down at Ryan. The youngster looked as if he wanted to follow his older brother, but he stayed at the fence watching Avery with a mixture of uncertainty and fascination.

Avery had the feeling he had been measured and found wanting. "I'm sorry I made Jenny cry."

"She doesn't like being called Jenny."

Unable to resist the urge to find out whatever this kid was willing to share about his sister, Avery took a step closer. "Why doesn't she like to be called Jenny?"

Didn't this make him guilty of the same conduct he'd rebuked Jennifer for? He was trying to gather information she wasn't willing to share with him. Would she be angry if she knew? Yeah, she would.

"Lizzie says it's because it was our dad's pet name for her and it makes Jennifer sad to think about him. I don't remember him because he died when I was a baby. Are you going to teach my sister how to use a gun? Can I shoot it, too?"

"No."

The boy frowned. "Why not?"

"The guns we use are not toys. They can hurt you."

Ryan sighed. "That's what Mom says. Do you want to see our rabbit? She isn't really our rabbit, she's Dr. Cutter's rabbit but we're keeping her for a while—only she has to stay in the barn now because she broke Mom's leg when Mom tried to step on her."

This kid not only looked like a small version of his sister, he talked like her, too. "Sounds like a dangerous character to me."

A mischievous grin appeared on the boy's face. "Mom or the rabbit?"

Avery chuckled. "My theory is that all women are dangerous characters."

"And mean. My sister Lizzie is always picking on me."

"Does Jenny, I mean Jennifer, pick on you?"

"No, but she makes me do chores and stuff. Come see Isabella." The boy walked to the gate in the fence and motioned for Avery to follow him.

Glancing at the house, Avery saw Jennifer come out the door. She now wore a full, floor-length yellow skirt. She hesitated as she caught sight of him watching, but after only a moment, she grasped the front of her outfit and lifted it enough to walk down the steps without tripping.

When she reached his side, she glared at him. "If you know what's good for you, Avery Barnes, you won't say a word. I know I look ridiculous."

He decided to take her advice and keep quiet, even though he didn't think she looked ridiculous at all.

She looked charming and very feminine in her old-fashioned costume. The flair of the yellow print skirt accentuated her small waist. The sway of the material as she walked and the peek of ruffled petticoat lace at her ankles did funny things to his insides.

"If you remember, I'm the one who goes around dressed as a Union trooper."

She brushed at her skirt. "True, but you and your men manage to look romantic in your uniforms."

Her eyes widened when she realized what she had said.

He hid a smile as he turned away. Oh, yes, at this rate, keeping their current arrangement strictly business was looking less likely by the minute.

Chapter Seven

Ryan didn't seem to notice the tension in the air between the two adults. The boy jumped up and down with pent-up excitement. "Avery wants to meet Isabella."

Jennifer relaxed when Avery didn't make any snide remarks about her outfit or her comment that he looked romantic. She hadn't meant to imply that she thought of Avery as romantic, but couldn't think how to explain herself without sounding even more foolish.

Happy to have a diversion, she smiled down at her brother. "Avery met Isabella when the army had Dakota at my hospital. Why don't you run along and play with Toby, or better yet, go keep Mom company?"

"But Avery wants to say hello to her. Don't you?"

Ryan looked so eager to show off his pet that Jennifer didn't have the heart to discourage him further. To her surprise, Avery said, "Sure, kid, I'd like to see your rabbit."

Jennifer shot him a grateful look.

"Great." Ryan took Avery's hand and began pulling him toward the barn. Once inside, he let go and dropped to his knees in front of a small wooden and wire mesh rabbit hutch.

"Wait a minute," Jennifer cautioned as she shut the barn door and carefully latched it. Inside the old building, dust motes danced in the air where the late afternoon sunshine cut rectangles of light into the dim interior. Fresh straw crackled underfoot and smelled of hot, dry summer days.

Ryan looked up at Avery. "We have to be careful. She might run away and get lost if she gets out, but I don't think she would. She likes it here."

Unlatching the cage door, he lifted the large brown bunny out and held her close.

Dropping to a crouch beside the boy, Avery stroked the rabbit's head. "I see you're still causing more trouble than you're worth."

He glanced up at Jennifer with a gleam in his eyes. "Do you remember how she had us all searching high and low at the clinic that day?"

Jennifer did. It had been the first day Avery had singled her out for attention. "I remember. She got out of her cage and went into Dakota's stall."

"I remember how mad Dr. Cutter was at Sergeant Mandel. He thought she was trying some new stress reduction therapy for her sick horse."

"He accused her of being harebrained. I had to straighten the two of them out. I thought for a minute I was going to have to send both of them to stand in the corner."

Ryan piped up. "Jennifer does that to me. I don't like it."

"Count yourself lucky," Avery said. "Brian and Lindsey wound up in more trouble than that."

"How much more?" Ryan asked, wide-eyed.

"A whole lot. They ended up getting married."

Looking uncertain, Ryan asked, "Is that bad?"

Avery nodded. "It's a fate worse than death."

"Don't tell him that," Jennifer said, glaring at Avery. Just when she found herself liking him again, he managed to remind her what a jerk he could be.

"I'm just teasing." He ruffled Ryan's hair and rose to his feet.

She spoke to her brother. "Put Isabella back in her pen and go get washed up."

"Aw, do I have to?"

"Yes. Mr. Barnes and I have work to do." She turned quickly, but stepped on her long hem and stumbled. Regaining her balance, she shot Avery a quelling look, gathered her skirting into a wad in front of her and left the barn.

Avery managed to keep the smile off his face until she was out of sight. He looked down at Ryan. The boy had his cheek resting on his furry friend's head.

"You'd better do as your sister says or she'll send us both to the corner."

"Okay." Ryan's reluctance was clear, but he did as he was told. When the bunny was safely secured, he climbed to his feet and started to leave the barn. It was then that Avery saw the mangled bicycle propped against the wall beside the door.

"Looks like someone had a wreck."

"My mom backed over it with her truck. Jennifer is going to get it fixed as soon as she has the money, but she has to pay for her school and bills first. The bike is a low pry—something."

"Priority?"

"I think so. Does that mean it's not very important?"

"Being stuck without wheels is never a low priority for a guy."

"That's what I think, but Jennifer says food on the table, a roof over our heads and feed for the animals come first." He did a fairly good falsetto imitation of his sister's voice and even managed to give that little shake of her shoulders she did when she was trying to be tough.

"Don't you believe that?"

"I guess I do. I know she and Mom worry a lot about bills. I hear them talking sometimes when I can't sleep."

A familiar sick sensation settled in the pit of Avery's stomach. He knew firsthand the lengths some women would go to solve their money problems. As much as he hated giving Edmond credit for anything, the truth was, his grandfather was the one who had opened Avery's eyes to that painful knowledge. "She should marry someone who is rich, then all her problems would be solved," he suggested bitterly.

"Lizzie says that, but Jennifer says she's only going to marry for love like Mom and Dad did."

Intrigued in spite of himself, Avery asked, "When did she say that?"

"Lots of times. I don't think being rich is a good thing."

"Why is that?" Avery asked.

"Because then you can't make your camel go through the eye of your needle." He shrugged his small shoulders. "Beats me why you'd want to, anyway."

Avery had to agree. Although he doubted Jennifer's little brother was privy to her true thoughts about marriage, it was oddly satisfying to know she at least paid lip service to marrying for love.

Thrusting aside his curiosity about Jennifer, he scrutinized the twisted metal. "It shouldn't take much to straighten the frame and get you a new front wheel."

"Could you fix it?" Ryan looked hopeful.

"Not without the right tools."

"Oh." The boy's disappointment was painfully clear.

"I know a couple of soldiers at the fort who work in the motor pool. They could fix it."

"Really? How much would that cost?"

"I'm not sure, but you and I could work out a deal."

Ryan tilted his head. "Like what?"

"Did you notice the spokes on my car's wheels?"

"They are, like, maximum sweet."

Avery tried not to laugh at the awe in the boy's voice. "I like them, too, but they're hard to keep clean. I'll get your bike fixed if you wash them for me once a week while I'm out here."

Ryan's eyes grew wide. "Sure."

"I don't mean just throw a little water on

them. I mean wash them inside and out, dry them and polish them so that they shine."

He nodded vigorously. "I can do that."

Avery smiled. "Then we have a deal. I'll bring the cleaning stuff with me when I come tomorrow. You'd better get going. Your sister and I have work to do."

As Avery left the barn with the boy, he saw Jennifer waiting for him beside his car. Walking up to her, he handed her the broomstick again. From the corner of his eye he saw her sister and brother come out of the house and park themselves on the front steps to watch.

"I still don't see what I'm going to learn with this," Jennifer said, an edge of annoyance in her voice.

"Hold it straight out in front of you."

She extended her arm. "Now what."

"Nothing. Hold it there until I tell you to put it down."

"This is silly."

He glanced at his wristwatch. "We'll see if you still think that after five minutes."

She stood rock solid for two full minutes before the tip of her stick began to wobble. After another minute a grimace appeared on her face, but she suppressed it when she noticed he was watching. Avery leaned against the front fender of his car and checked his watch again. "Two more minutes."

The tip wavered even more. "I don't see how this will help me hit a target."

"Yes, you do."

"Okay, I'll admit this is showing me which muscles I'll need to strengthen."

"Very good. And?"

Her arm dropped to her side. "It shows me that you like to watch me suffer."

He tapped his watch. "You still have a minute left."

She glared at him but raised her arm again. "How often should I do this?"

"At least ten times a day."

"That won't be so bad."

"I'm not done yet. Today, you can practice with the stick alone, but tomorrow I want you to start adding weight to it."

"How much weight?"

"The sabers we use weigh about eight pounds."

She dropped her arm again and stared at him open-mouthed. "You've got to be kidding. You want me to hold eight pounds out in front of myself for five minutes?"

"Among other things, yes. You have thirty seconds left."

With a long suffering sigh, she extended her arm. "What other things?"

"You're going to study the parts of a saber and of a pistol."

"Why? I'm going to do this stunt one time. I can pretty much promise you that once it's over I'm never touching a saber or a gun again."

"You have to become familiar with the tools you're going to be using. They can be very dangerous in the hands of someone who doesn't understand them. I assume you don't want to injure yourself or anyone else."

"Of course not."

"Did you know that cavalry horses were often shot and killed by their own inept riders?"

"Really?" She glanced at him. The expression on her face was a mixture of distress and disbelief.

He nodded. "Really."

"But I'll be using blanks."

"Blanks still require a charge of black powder that can make a nasty burn or even blind your mount. You can put your arm down now."

She dropped the stick and rubbed her shoulder. He asked, "Are you okay?"

"Remind me to have you spend five minutes holding up your horse before you start your riding lessons."

Chuckling, he said, "That will be easier than trying to hold up the instructor."

Her brother's hearty laughter rang out. Avery kept his eyes on Jennifer's expressive face. It took a second for his teasing comment to sink in. When it did, her jaw dropped.

She punched his shoulder. "I can't believe you said that. I do not weigh as much as a horse. You take it back."

"Fat chance." Ducking away from her outrage, he chuckled as he spun around to put the hood of his car between them.

"Get him, Jen," Lizzie called out.

"Look out, she pinches," Ryan yelled.

His sister elbowed him. "Whose side are you on?"

Jennifer advanced on Avery, a mischievous gleam in her eyes. "I said take it back."

"Or what? You'll make me sorry?" he taunted and took a step back.

"Yes." She lunged toward him, but her feet tangled in her long hem and she fell.

He jumped forward and managed to catch her against his chest. The weight of her slight body in his arms triggered an avalanche of emotions.

Protectiveness, tenderness, an overwhelming desire to kiss her took his breath away. So much for keeping his emotions under control. She looked up at him, her eyes wide with shock. Did she feel it, too? Her lips parted ever so slightly. He bent his head to kiss her.

Chapter Eight

Jennifer came to her senses an instant before Avery's lips touched hers and turned her face aside. What kind of fool was she to let this man toy with her emotions again? Hadn't she learned her lesson the first time?

Steadying herself, she quickly regained her footing and stepped back. His hands dropped from her arms and he asked, "Are you okay?"

Did his voice sound breathless or was it her imagination? Why did his aftershave have to smell so good? Why did his touch have to send her heart racing? Wasn't she ever going to get over him? It had been such a bad idea to ask him here.

"I'm fine," she stated, holding her head up and forcing old dreams from her mind. "I guess lesson number two should be how to walk in one of these dresses."

"I'm afraid I can't help you with that."

She managed a small smile and hoped it covered how rattled she was. "I'd give a day's wages to see you try."

"Not a chance."

From the front steps, Lizzie yelled, "Mom says to stand up straight and take small steps."

Jennifer took a deep breath and blew it out slowly. "At least no one in the family missed me making a fool of myself."

A twitch at the corner of Avery's mouth told her he was trying not to laugh. "Tomorrow I'll bring a saber and scabbard so you can practice walking with that in addition to your petticoats."

"Goody, goody. I can't wait. Are we done here or do we have more stick work?"

"You're ready to try riding while keeping that broomstick in your right hand."

He stepped around her and opened the car door. "I also brought this for you." He withdrew a red folder and handed it to her. "Your study guide."

She tucked the folder under her arm. "Fine. Now it's your turn. Did you bring your saddle?"

"It's in the trunk."

"Get it and come along." With her chin up, she proceeded with shortened strides to the corral behind the barn where McCloud and Lollypop stood patiently waiting for riders.

She stopped beside her gray gelding and rubbed his cheek. After a few minutes, Avery joined her and hefted his McClellen saddle to the top rail of the fence.

He moved to stand at her elbow. "Your gelding is a good-looking fellow."

She wished Avery wouldn't hover so close. It made it hard to think straight. "Thank you. This is McCloud. He's going to help me show you the finer points of horsemanship. The black mare is Lollypop, my mother's horse. She'll be carrying me on my charge as she is apparently already gun trained. I really had no idea how much effort my mother had been putting into this affair."

Hearing a commotion overhead, both Jennifer and Avery looked up. Jennifer's siblings were positioning themselves in the open hayloft doorway. Toby sat with his legs dangling out while Lizzie and Ryan stretched out on their stomachs with their chins propped on their hands.

Avery wagged his eyebrows. "Chaperones?"

"Ignore them. I find that works best. Mount up, soldier. Let's see what you've got."

She ducked under the horse's neck, stumbled on her skirt again, but managed to recover without falling on her face.

These clothes were ridiculous. How on earth had women functioned in long skirts for centuries? Glancing over her shoulder, she was relieved to see Avery was busy saddling the horse and hadn't noticed another less than graceful episode. Opening the gate to the corral, she stood beside it as he led McCloud through.

"What now?" he asked.

"Lead him a quarter way into the arena and halt. Make sure he is standing square, then mount. I want to see you walk once around, then move to a trot for one round followed by a canter."

Standing with her hands on her hips, she watched him follow her instructions, mount and set McCloud into motion. Her trained eye followed his progress, cataloging problems and formulating a plan to address them. As much as she hated to admit it, he looked good on horseback.

Like that was a surprise. He always looked good. His jeans and long-sleeved gray T-shirt didn't hide the fact that he was fit and well muscled. He wore his modern clothing well, but handsome wasn't even the word for the romantic picture he made when he wore his cavalry uniform.

In her mind's eye she saw him with his saber flashing in the sunlight as he and his fellow soldiers brought history alive in their performances. No wonder the legend of the dashing cavalry soldier still lived in the hearts and minds of people everywhere. If only she could get *her* romance with Avery out of her heart and mind.

Biting her lip, she refused to follow where that train of thought was leading. A handsome face and a well-toned body didn't have anything to do with being a truly good man.

After finishing her instructions, he pulled McCloud to a halt in front of her. He patted the horse's neck. "He's a sweet goer. So what did you think? I'm pretty good, right?"

She told the truth. "You're an average rider."

He sat back and scowled. "What?"

"Okay, you're a good rider, but you're trying to overpower your horse. This event is about harmony between a horse and rider. It's about lightness and relaxation."

"It's also about military bearing and confidence."

"Those you don't need to work on. You have pompous and arrogant down to a science."

"And you've got a master's in peevish."

Taken aback, she said, "I beg your pardon?"

"You should." His tone was so smug she didn't know if she could control herself.

She threw out her arm and pointed at the gate.

"If you aren't serious about learning this, get off my horse and go back to the fort."

"Play nice, children," Lizzie called down from the loft.

"Yes," Avery chimed in. "Play nice, Jenny. We both have a lot at stake."

Jennifer glanced from her sister back to Avery. He was right. She had made a promise to her mother. The only way she knew to keep it was to put up with Avery's cockiness.

"All right, I'll play nice but I don't have to like it. Take McCloud down the left side of the corral at a trot and then into a ten meter circle in the center. While you're at it, pay attention to him. He's the one who *does* know what he's doing."

Avery nudged the horse closer and leaned down so only Jennifer could hear. "You're really cute when you're mad. Did you know that?"

Avery's remark succeeded in silencing Jennifer for the rest of the session, except for a few pointed riding instructions from her. His comment had been designed to do exactly that, but he hadn't been lying. She was adorable when she was miffed.

It was too dangerous to give in to the temptation to hold her in his arms and kiss her soft lips, but he'd settle for seeing the icy sparks in her bright blue eyes. Besides, if his teasing kept her at a distance, so much the better. He had no intention of getting emotionally tangled up with her again.

After an hour, she declared the lesson at an end. The sun was getting low in the sky, turning the few bands of clouds in the sky a pale pink.

"That's enough for today." Her tone was cool and clearly meant to sound professional.

Dismounting near the fence, Avery gave McCloud a final pat and unhooked the girth. When he pulled the saddle off, Jennifer came forward and took the reins in her hand. "I'll take him now."

"You don't trust me to cool him down?" Avery challenged.

He waited for her snippy comeback, but she surprised him by saying, "Actually, when it comes to caring for horses, I do trust you. I've seen you in action at the clinic and at the stables. You're good with animals. It's just that McCloud is my buddy and I like to take care of him."

Avery basked in the unexpected warmth of her compliment. "Thanks. Aren't you going to practice with your broomstick on Lollypop now?"

"I think I'll wait until after I've changed out of

this skirt. I've appeared foolish enough in front of an audience for one day. I'll see you tomorrow."

"Same time?"

"That's what we agreed on. Every day at four-thirty for the next two weeks."

"I'll be here. Don't forget to study the stuff I gave you." He found he didn't want to leave, but he couldn't think of a reason to stay.

As he walked with slow steps back to his car with his saddle over his arm, Ryan raced up to his side. "You're still going to get my bike fixed, aren't you?"

"Sure, kid."

"I'll get it for you." The boy ran back the way they had come.

Avery aimed his keyless remote at the trunk and the lid popped open. Laying his riding gear inside, he turned to see Ryan struggling to carry his wrecked bicycle across the yard. Avery moved quickly to intercept him and relieve the boy of his burden.

"How long do you think it will take to fix it? Do you think it'll be ready by tomorrow?"

Shaking his head, Avery said, "Probably not tomorrow."

"The next day?" Shoving his hands in the front pockets of his jeans, Ryan bit the corner of his lip.

"I doubt it, but I'll put a rush order on it."

"Thanks. Don't worry about my sister."

Avery closed the trunk. "What do you mean?"

"Jennifer gets all mad and huffy sometimes like she did today, but she gets over it quick. Toby says you just have to give her space and look kinda sorry."

"You just have to look sorry, you don't have to be sorry?"

Ryan leaned toward him. "That's what Toby says, but I think she can tell the difference."

"I'll remember that. See you tomorrow, kid." Avery looked toward the barn but Jennifer didn't appear. Realizing how much he wanted to see her again made him turn abruptly and get into his car.

The following afternoon, Jennifer rushed to get supper started before Avery arrived. Lately it seemed as if she were trying to stuff twenty-eight hours of work, classes and chores into a twenty-four hour day, only now she had to add two more hours of instructions each evening to the mix.

From her place in front of the kitchen sink, she heard the front door open. "Ryan, is that you?"

"Yup."

"Did you feed Isabella?"

"Oops, I forgot."

"Please do it now."

"Okay. You stay here. I'll be right back." The sound of the door slamming made her roll her eyes. That boy was always on the run.

"I'm done," Toby announced. Seated at the kitchen table, he closed his social studies book and slid it into his book bag.

"Good, then you can help me study." Jennifer blew a wisp of hair out of her face as she finished chopping carrots into bite-size pieces and started on the potatoes.

"Ask me some questions about equine podiatry. I've got a test tomorrow. My textbook is there beside you."

Jennifer added the diced carrots and potatoes to the pan containing the pot roast, then began to slice the onions on the wooden cutting board on the kitchen counter.

Toby opened her book. After a few seconds, he said, "Describe three ways to manage a horse with a toe crack."

Jennifer tried to concentrate, but all she could think about was seeing Avery soon. Her eagerness to see him again made her wonder if she needed her head examined. She forced her mind back to her studies. "Three methods of treatment are acrylic repair…hoof staples…and…I can't remember."

"The use of a metal band with screws." Toby supplied the answer she couldn't pull out of her brain.

The sound of the dryer buzzer reached her. Jennifer stopped slicing and shouted, "Lizzie, can you hang up my lab coats for me before they get wrinkled, please?"

"I'll get the laundry," Mary called from her bedroom.

"Stay in bed, Mother." Jennifer yelled back. "Lizzie, please? I'm in the middle of making supper."

"Okay—I'll get them," Lizzie called back, vague annoyance clear in her tone.

Toby asked, "What are the advantages of using a treatment plate on a punctured hoof?"

Jennifer closed her eyes and tried to focus. It didn't do any good. "Advantages of a treatment plate include less bandage changes…and something else."

"Increased ease of observation." Toby enunciated each word with care.

"Oh, that's right." Looking down, she finished slicing the onion just as her eyes began to water. Adding the white rings to the pan, she seasoned the roast then opened the warm oven and slid the pan in, taking care to keep her mother's long skirt from getting shut in the door.

The costumes were a hassle, but her mother was right. The more she wore the period dresses the more natural moving in them became.

She rubbed her nose with the back of one hand. The pungent odor made her realize she smelled like onions. She moved to the kitchen sink, squirted lemon dish soap on her hands and scrubbed.

"How do you make one?" Toby asked.

Jennifer dried her hands on a dish towel, then flipped it over her shoulder. What else needed doing?

"How do you make one?" Toby asked again.

"How do I make what?" she snapped. Sniffing her fingers, she frowned. Now she smelled like lemon-scented onions.

Her brother shook his head. "I don't think you're gonna do so well on this test, sis."

She threw him an exasperated look. "Ask me something else."

"What are the parts of a saber?" a deep, masculine voice queried from the doorway of the living room.

She spun around to see Avery leaning casually against the door frame.

"What are you doing here?"

"I'm just waiting on you." Avery enjoyed the stunned look on her face. Her cheeks were flushed, and damp tendrils of hair curled at her temples. She had on another frontier style dress. This one was baby blue with tiny red flowers scattered across the fabric and red cord trim. The colors suited her.

Embarrassed at being caught off guard, she said, "I didn't hear you knock."

"I came in with Ryan. He told me to wait here while he fed the rabbit."

"Oh." She bit the corner of her lower lip. She looked rushed and flustered and a lot like a woman with too much on her plate.

Watching her interact with her family unobserved had been enlightening for him. She managed to get her siblings to help her and each other with only a small amount of encouragement and prodding. Her home, which he once would have considered shabby, struck him as a warm and comfortable place. He'd never known anything like it.

"I've hung up the laundry. Do you need help with anything else?" Lizzie came into the room and stopped short at the sight of Avery.

"Don't let me interrupt your work," he said, smiling at Jennifer.

She snatched the dish towel off her shoulder and clutched it in her hands, then tossed it on the counter top. "I'm done here. Let me tell

Mom and make sure she is okay, then we can go outside."

"You didn't answer my question," he said as he stepped aside for her to pass.

"What question was that?"

"What are the parts of a saber?"

"The toe, which is really the point, the grip, the guard and the blade. The scabbard is comprised of the mouth, the upper hook, the lower hook, the body and the scabbard tip protector." She rattled off the list with barely a pause.

Toby snapped the book shut. "That might impress him, but it isn't going to get you through your equine podiatry exam."

Jennifer pulled her textbook from Toby's hands. "I'm not trying to impress anyone. I'll read the chapter again tonight. Would you check and see if Mom needs anything?"

"I'm fine," Mary called from the bedroom. "You kids should go outside and play."

"Yes, Mom," Lizzie and Toby answered together as they exchanged pointed looks.

Jennifer rolled her eyes. Avery tried not to smile. It was obvious that having her siblings lined up and watching her every move wasn't what she wanted. The door burst open and Ryan came running in.

"I'm sure you kids would rather watch TV or play your video games," Jennifer suggested.

"Not me," Ryan announced. "I've got stuff to do for Avery. Right?"

"Right," Avery agreed and the boy raced out the front door again.

Jennifer followed more sedately. On the porch, she gathered a handful of the floor-length skirt she was wearing and descended the steps carefully. She was definitely getting the hang of moving in her mother's period costumes.

Ryan was dragging the garden hose from the side of the house toward Avery's car. "I got the hose."

Jennifer glanced from her brother to Avery. "What does Ryan need the hose for?"

"He's going to wash and polish my spoke wheels for me."

"Why?"

"It's a deal between us guys. The cloth and polish are on the front seat. Make sure you get all the water spots off."

"I will." Ryan aimed the pressure nozzle at the car and let loose a wide arc of spray.

Avery winced. There would be water spots on more than the wheel covers. He foresaw an evening of hand polishing his pride and joy all over again.

Jennifer glared at Avery, her hands fisted on her hips. "Are you taking advantage of my little brother?"

"No, and I'm ashamed you would even ask that. Are you ready for your next lesson?"

"Certainly."

"Good. Kill the water, sport."

"Yes, sir. I'll get a bucket." Ryan shouted and took his hand off the nozzle.

Avery opened the car door and pulled out a scabbard. "Strap this on."

Jennifer took it from his hand and buckled the belt around her waist. "I still don't see why I have to learn to walk with this thing."

"Because the only safe way to carry a saber is in a scabbard. This is for the welfare of the other re-enactors as much as it is for you. Stop arguing for one minute and do as I say."

"I'm not arguing."

"Yes, you are."

"I am not. Is this right?" She shifted the long weapon to her left side.

"A little farther back." He bent and adjusted it for her. "Do you smell onions?"

She clasped her hands behind her back. "No."

The sound of the front door slamming drew his attention and Jennifer took a step away. Ryan came out of the house carrying a pail.

Lizzie and Toby came out and sat on the top step to watch the activity. As the boy set to work scrubbing the first wheel, Avery turned back to Jennifer. "Try walking a few paces."

Jennifer took several steps toward the house. The saber banged awkwardly against her leg. She stopped, then took several more steps with the same results. She grasped the hilt to steady it and glanced at Avery, daring him to laugh.

He folded his arms across his chest. "It's a lot harder than it looks, isn't it?"

"How does Kevin Costner make it look so easy?"

"Practice."

She turned and walked a few paces in the other direction. "Can I keep one hand on the hilt to steady it?"

"For now. Spend a few more minutes just walking and then you can work on sitting with it on."

She walked to the barn and back. "The weight makes a person want to swagger. It's empowering."

"Therein lies the true lure of swordplay for centuries past."

"Does it make you feel the same way?"

"I feel more empowered with a machine gun in my hands, but I know what you mean."

She grasped the hilt and pulled the blade free, holding it in front of her. "Wow. It's a lot heavier than a broomstick. Did I get all the parts right?"

"You did."

She tried several times to insert the tip of the blade back into the scabbard, but kept missing. Avery stepped up, placed his hands over hers and guided the sword home. The feel of her small hand beneath his sent his pulse racing. She drew in a quick breath as her eyes met his. His hands lingered a moment longer.

"Avery!" Ryan shouted. "I got this wheel done. Come and see."

Smiling at Jennifer, Avery said softly, "I should go and inspect his work."

"Yes." She sounded breathless. Was he the reason?

"I'll only be a minute," he added as he moved away.

A minute might not be long enough, he decided as his heartbeat settled to a more normal pace once he wasn't touching her.

He pointed out a few spots that Ryan had missed in his cleaning frenzy, then followed Jennifer with his eyes as she paced back and forth across the gravel drive.

She was smart, sassy, easy on the eyes. She was a woman of principles. The kind who put faith and family first. In other words, she was exactly the kind of woman he wanted to avoid. So why did he find himself drawn to her? He didn't have the answer and it bothered him.

Jennifer walked toward the barn and practiced sitting on a bale of straw beside the door. Managing both the long skirt and the saber took a little finesse, but she was happy to be able to concentrate on something other than her reaction to Avery's touch.

When he walked toward her a few minutes later, she leapt to her feet and unbuckled the sword. Holding it toward him, she said. "It's time we started working on your training. I'll go get the horses."

"You need to sit straighter in the saddle. Move your shoulders forward to center your weight over your hips. Relax, you look like a stick up there."

Avery pulled his mount to a halt and glared at Jennifer sitting perched on the corral fence. She had taken off her skirt and was wearing a pair of well-worn jeans.

"You just told me to sit up straight and now you're telling me to relax. Which is it?"

"Both."

"You're not making any sense." Not only

were her instructions contradictory, but her presence was proving to be a distraction that was hard to ignore. Very hard.

"Try not to think of this as a military exercise. Try to think of this as having fun," she suggested. "Become an extension of the horse instead of a lump perched on top of him."

Exasperated, he shot back, "I'm pretty sure military equitation isn't about having fun. It's about having control of the horse."

"The two are not mutually exclusive. Step down and I'll show you what I mean."

Avery dismounted as Jennifer hopped down from the fence and joined him. He flipped up the saddle leather and began shortening the stirrup for her. They had been at this for over an hour and so far all he had accomplished was feeling like an inept novice.

When he finished shortening the second stirrup, he gave her a leg up and stepped back. With an almost imperceptible nudge of her heels, she set McCloud into motion.

Avery's annoyance evaporated as he watched her ride in a wide circle around him. She and the horse moved with almost flawless grace. She made it look so easy.

"Don't try to overwhelm the horse with control," she said. "If you look at your mount as a true partner, you'll both do better. See how relaxed his stride has become?"

"He's used to you."

She reined to a stop beside Avery. "You're making excuses, but you do have a point."

Kicking free of the stirrups, she dropped lightly to the ground and patted McCloud's neck. "Why don't you take him for a ride down the lane?"

"Are we done?"

"Think of it as recess. It will help both of you because it isn't work. McCloud deserves a little fun, too, and for him that's a good gallop."

Avery closed his hand over hers where she held the reins. "I'll go if you'll join me." It was a rash and risky move, but he couldn't help himself. He wanted to spend time alone with her again.

She pulled her fingers free slowly. A blush colored her cheeks. Stepping back a pace, she shoved her hands in the hip pockets of her jeans. "I should get started on my homework. I've got a big test coming up."

He turned his back on her and began lengthening the stirrups again. "I can understand why you might not trust yourself to go riding alone with me."

"What's that supposed to mean?"

"Nothing."

"No, you were implying something."

"Only that it would just be the two of us and your family wouldn't be scrutinizing your every move." He gestured toward the corral fence with his head. Toby, Lizzie and Ryan were seated on the top rail watching them.

"If you are suggesting that I'll find you impossible to resist once I'm away from prying eyes—you're delusional."

"If you're afraid you can't control yourself, the best thing is to admit it."

"I'm not afraid."

"Guess we'll never know for sure, will we? That's a pity since it would be so easy to prove."

Chapter Nine

"All right," Jennifer stated. "I'll accompany you on a ride but only because my mother's horse needs exercising."

Avery had his back to her but he could easily imagine the way her stubborn little chin would jut out as she accepted his challenge. He controlled his grin with difficulty. "I'll wait here while you saddle up."

"I'll only be a minute."

"I thought you were going to study for your test," Toby said from the sidelines, glaring at Avery.

"I will. You kids can go in and get ready for supper." Jennifer patted Toby's knee as she walked past him and into the barn.

"I'll wait here," Toby replied and crossed his arms.

Avery had to admire the boy's determined guardianship of his sister, even if she didn't need it.

Jennifer came out of the barn with Lollypop a few seconds later. Grabbing a handful of mane, she swung up onto the mare's bare back and rode up to the gate. She pulled the bolt back and let the gate swing open. Looking at Avery, she said, "Are you coming?"

"Lead on."

Kicking Lollypop into a canter, she took off down the drive. McCloud whinnied as his stablemate left without him. Avery swung into the saddle. He didn't have to urge McCloud to catch up. By the time they reached the end of the lane, the horses were side by side.

Stopping at the narrow paved road, Jennifer checked for oncoming traffic, then crossed the highway. The horses' hooves clattered loudly on the blacktop. Once across, Jennifer led the way through a break in the trees that lined the roadway.

Avery ducked beneath the gnarled thorny branches of the Osage orange hedge. Beyond the trees a large field opened up. The corn crop had already been harvested from it leaving long rows of pale stubble and a few occasional brown stalks waving in the wind.

Jennifer urged her mount into an easy lope

toward the tree covered hills rising at the far end of the field. McCloud proved eager to stretch his legs. Soon both horses were pounding across the open ground with only the sounds of their hooves hitting the soft dirt and the occasional crackle of trampled stalks disturbing the evening quiet.

Avery found himself torn between watching his riding companion and helping his horse find his way across the field. Jennifer looked so carefree, so happy as she sat astride the black mare flying over the ground. For a brief second, he caught her with her eyes closed as she lifted her face to the wind. All too soon the distance had been covered and the horses slowed.

At the edge of the field, Jennifer pulled to a walk and cast a grin at Avery. "I needed that."

"You could have just told your family that you wanted to get away from the house and have a good gallop," he suggested, pulling his blowing horse alongside hers.

She sent him a quick glance, then bent to pat Lollypop's neck. The blush in her cheeks might have been from the wind, but he couldn't be sure. No matter what the reason, it heightened her beauty.

"Thanks for giving me an excuse to do it," she said, ignoring his suggestion. "Since Toby and Lizzie have decided it's their duty to chaperone us, I've been feeling like the microbe under the microscope."

"My pleasure. Why not just tell your family you need some time to yourself?" he asked, not willing to let the point drop.

She drew her fingers through the mare's long black mane. "I guess it's partly that I don't like to complain."

"And the other part?"

She wrinkled her nose. "I don't like to admit that I can't do it all."

"Why do you think you need to do it all?"

"Mom has more than enough to worry about. She knows that if she needs surgery it will take most of our savings and it will mean I'll have to drop out of school for this semester. I don't know how much longer we can get along without her income as it is."

"Are you serious?" He knew how hard she studied, how much she wanted to finish school and start supporting her family.

Shrugging her dainty shoulders, she said, "It is what it is. I'm trusting that God has a plan for us."

"What if the plan is something you don't like?"

"I'm human. I'll be disappointed. I'll cry. I'll yell. Then I'll make peace with it because that is what I believe. God is in control. I'm not."

"I don't like the idea that I'm not in control of my life."

"Yes, that is one hard part of our faith, but believing that God is in control doesn't mean we live without direction. I have things I want. Things I plan for and work toward. I want my mother to get better, I want to stay in school and I want to make her proud by re-enacting her heroine's part in history without falling on my face."

"You'll do okay with your charge up Strawberry Hill."

"Dutton Heights," she corrected.

"Whatever. You'll do okay." He relaxed and took a deep breath of the clean evening air. This was nice, riding beside her, talking about things that were important to her.

Shaking her head, she said, "I don't know how you can say that when you have yet to let me hold a saber while I'm on horseback."

"You're determined to do well. That's three-fifths of the battle. Why is this whole thing so important to your mother?"

"I wish I knew. Why is winning the Sheridan cup so important to you?"

"It's not."

McCloud shied as a pheasant flew up ahead of them, and Avery spoke quietly to calm to the horse. Once again Jennifer was struck by how patient he was with animals. If only he treated people as well.

Was the arrogant rich snob the real Avery or was he the dedicated soldier and kindhearted man she sometimes caught a glimpse of? What did his relationship with his grandfather have to do with his behavior?

Uncovering the real Avery Barnes was a tempting idea. One she couldn't easily dismiss. Although she had promised herself she could maintain a strictly business attitude toward him, she found that resolve faltering.

The horses seemed content to amble along together, their tails twitching at the occasional buzzing fly. Jennifer glanced at Avery from beneath her lashes as she narrowed her eyes. "I think winning the cup is very important to you. It has something to do with your grandfather, doesn't it?"

"You're getting nosey again, Jenny," he warned.

She didn't care if he was annoyed. Somehow, she knew it was important for him to talk about his grandfather. "So sue me. He seems like a nice old man."

"Don't let the dapper charm fool you. He has a heart of flint."

She accepted the finality of his tone, but

rather than dropping the subject, she tried a different approach. "What was it like?"

"What was what like?"

"Growing up with money, privilege, prominent social status?"

"What was it like to grow up underprivileged?" he countered.

She tilted her head as she considered her answer. "It was ordinary. It was great. I never lacked for anything. I knew my parents loved me. I knew my grandparents adored me. I can't think of a better way to grow up. I think my one real worry has always been that I might disappoint them somehow."

"You don't know how lucky you are. I knew my parents hated each other, but they both loved money enough to stay together. I knew my grandfather has always considered me a weakling and a fool."

A sharp stab of sympathy made her breath catch in her throat. "Why would you say that?"

For a long moment, she thought he wasn't going to answer her. When he did, his voice held a hard edge. "I had asthma when I was younger than Ryan. I was in and out of hospitals constantly for the first six years of my life. Fortunately, I outgrew it, but from the time I was born I was a disappointment to the old man who wanted another strong and ruthless heir to run his empire."

"Is that why you try so hard to make people think you don't care?"

"I *don't* care. I'm a carefree fellow. Ask anyone who knows me and they'll tell you the same."

"I saw the way you worked to help rehab Dakota. I've never seen you make light of the army or of your unit's mission. You do care. You care about your friends."

"I have made some good friends in the army," he admitted. "Basic training is a great leveler of men. Crawling beneath strands of barbed wire with bullets from a live machine gun zinging overhead can make you appreciate the people around you in a whole new way."

"Do they really make you do that?"

"That and a whole lot more."

"Wasn't it scary?"

"I think that was the point."

She closed her eyes. "The most scared I have ever been was at my father's funeral."

Jennifer wasn't sure why she needed to share her darkest hour with Avery. Perhaps because she sensed he would understand how alone she'd felt that day. "I was afraid I wouldn't be brave enough for him and for my mother. She took it so hard when he died."

"What happened to him?"

"He had a brain tumor. He died less than five weeks after he was diagnosed. Mother just sat in his chair and cried for days. If it hadn't been for my grandmother, I don't know what would have happened to us. She came in and took over until my mother found her way back from her grief. What happened to your parents?"

"Small plane crash. My dad was a pilot. Mom hated to fly with him. She always said he was reckless, but she went with him that day because they were flying out to Nassau and she loved it there."

Both parents at once. How horrible that must have been for him. "How old were you?"

"Sixteen. How old were you?"

"Fourteen."

He met her gaze. "How did you get through it?"

"My faith got me through it. I kept imagining Dad and God having this great, long conversation. When he was alive, whenever there was something my dad didn't understand, he'd say, 'I'm going to ask God about that when I get to heaven.' What got you through your parents' funeral?"

"Anger."

"At who?"

"God. Fate. My grandfather. He took only

one day off work for the funeral. After that, he headed back to his empire and left me wondering what was next."

"Not everyone grieves in the same way," she said softly.

"Some people don't grieve at all," he shot back, a dry, bitter twist in his tone.

A fresh breeze kicked up and Jennifer noticed storm clouds gathering in the west. Reluctantly, she turned her horse toward home. "Perhaps your grandfather is here now because he has regrets?" she suggested.

Avery eyed her intently. "Why do you say that?"

She wanted to tell him that his grandfather was ill, that he might not have much time, but she knew it wasn't her place. She swallowed the words. "I don't know. Why do you think he's here?"

"I think he got bored without me to insult back in Boston."

"And if you are wrong about that?"

He fixed his eyes straight ahead. "Trust me, I'm not."

"You might consider the fact that God brought him here for a reason. Forgiveness heals the forgiver as well as the forgiven."

"That sounds like some of your church

mumbo jumbo. I thought you weren't going to try and push your faith down my throat."

"I never said I wasn't going to give you good advice."

A smile tugged at the corner of his mouth, but he managed to subdue it. "Is this Jennifer's top ten tips to positive living?"

"I can't take credit for the basic idea. God suggested it first."

"Give it up, Jenny. I'm a lost soul. You can't reform me."

"You're right. I can't—but I know that God can."

Chapter Ten

Later, as Avery drove back to his apartment, he tried without success to dismiss Jennifer and her family from his mind.

He had known she didn't come from money like he did, but seeing firsthand the simple way they lived had forged a new respect for her. She attended school full-time, worked almost as many hours at the clinic and still managed to help her mother care for the younger children.

He wasn't sure he could do half as much. The odd thing was, in all the time he had known her, he'd never heard her complain. She never acted as though her life were anything but joyful. How did she manage that?

Turning into the parking lot of his complex, he followed the winding drive to the last building. Low gray clouds were moving in quickly and the first few raindrops splattered on his windshield just before he pulled into his allotted space. Getting out, he sprinted toward his front door with his key in hand.

A tall shade tree surrounded by a black circular metal bench graced the center of the small court-yard outside his building. He saw the man sitting there, but paid little attention as he dashed to the portico over his front door. He had his key in the lock when he heard someone call his name.

Looking over his shoulder, he saw the man from the bench rise. Avery recognized his grandfather and his stomach clenched. "What are you doing here?"

"I was hoping to have a few words with you," Edmond said.

"I don't have anything to say to you."

Shoulders hunched against the cool drizzle, Edmond stepped away from the bench. "Then could I use your phone? I dismissed my driver."

Disgusted with the tug of sympathy he felt, Avery asked, "What's the matter with your cell phone?"

"The battery seems to be dead. Charging it appears to be one of the many things my secretary usually does for me that I fail to notice. I believe I shall have to give her a raise."

It had begun raining in earnest by this time.

Avery pushed open his door and tipped his head in that direction.

"Thank you." Edmond walked past him and entered, stopping in the small foyer. Pulling a white silk handkerchief from the inner pocket of his suit coat, he wiped his face.

"How long have you been sitting out there?"

Edmond returned the cloth square to his pocket, then rubbed his hands together for warmth. "Two hours. I took a chance that you would be here after your regular duty hours."

"Must be odd for you to find out you can be mistaken. The phone is on the wall in the kitchen."

"Thank you."

As Edmond made his call, Avery took a few minutes to change into a clean T-shirt and dark blue running pants, and exchange his riding boots for a pair of sneakers. When he walked back into the living area, Edmond was sitting on one of the kitchen chairs.

It surprised Avery how tired and worn Edmond looked. He remembered his grandfather as a powerful and dynamic man, always on the go and impatient of people without his energy. Edmond rubbed his hands together again. "Collin went back to the inn. It will take him about twenty minutes to return. I could wait outside if that would make you more comfortable."

"How did you find me?"

"Let's just say I have resources."

Avery remembered the dark SUV that seemed to be everywhere he was. "You hired a private eye to follow me."

"Yes."

"You're unbelievable."

"You left me with very little choice."

Avery walked past him into the kitchen. Picking up the coffeemaker carafe, he turned to the sink and began filling it with water. "Your coat is wet."

Edmond brushed at his sleeves. "A small matter compared to my only grandson's hatred."

Avery stood staring at the water running over the sides of the container. Time had dulled the pain of his grandfather's betrayal, but not erased it. "I don't hate you."

"But you haven't forgiven me," Edmond stated.

Turning away from the sink, Avery transferred the water into the machine, glad to be able to focus on something other than the jumble of emotions he was feeling. "Why are you here?"

"There are things you and I need to discuss."

"Have you decided to cut me out of your will all together?" It was easier to be flippant than face the things he really wanted to say.

"Would it matter to you if I did?"

"Probably."

"At least that's an honest answer."

Avery pulled a bag of gourmet coffee from the fridge, opened it, and spooned the grounds into the filter basket. The rich soothing scent of his favorite blend filled the air.

Edmond slipped his coat off and hung it over the back of his chair. For the next few minutes, the only sound in the small room was the sputter and gurgle of the coffeemaker. Finally, Edmond said, "You have a nice apartment. I didn't know enlisted men were allowed to live off post."

"With the return of the Big Red One, barrack space is limited. All it took was getting permission from my commanding officer."

"I've met Captain Watson. He seems like a good man."

Avery scowled at him. "When did you talk to the captain?"

"This afternoon before coming here."

"You can't stay out of my affairs, can you?"

"Miranda was a gold digger. She was after your money. What's more, she was an impatient gold digger. She could have had much more than I offered her if she had been willing to wait until you were married, but she wanted the money in a hurry."

"I was made painfully aware of that by your interference."

"I know you think what I did was wrong, but I did it for the right reasons."

"Did you try to buy off my mother before she married Dad?"

Edmond raised his chin. "I didn't, but perhaps I should have. I wanted my son to be happy. He was wildly in love with her—for a while. Like you, he found someone who loved money more than she loved him. She made his life miserable. I wasn't about to watch that happen to you."

"Why did he stay with her if he was that miserable?" Avery remembered the screaming fights, the tears and accusations. They echoed in his head whenever he thought about settling down and spending his life with one person. Miranda had been able to silence the sounds of his childhood and he had loved her for that.

Only her whispered words of love had been as much a lie as his parents' sham of a marriage.

"Your father stayed with your mother because of you."

"Great. Now you're trying to lay their unhappy marriage at my feet. As far as you're concerned, I've never done anything right, including being born."

"That isn't true."

His grandfather expected him to be a failure at everything. Well, he knew exactly how to do that. He'd had years of practice. Avery brushed past Edmond and snatched his car keys from the end of the counter. "I used to wonder why you made it your mission in life to belittle and embarrass me and now I know. Thanks for this heart-to-heart, Gramps. Enjoy the coffee. I'm sure you can find your way out."

Avery left the apartment, slamming the door as he headed into the rain.

Jennifer closed her textbook of equine anatomy and glanced at the silent phone for the hundredth time since she'd gotten home. It was Friday evening and she had turned down an extra shift at the clinic to work with Avery, but he was nowhere in sight.

He hadn't shown up at the prearranged time. Nor had he bothered to call. They had agreed to meet at the same time every evening for two weeks. Where was he? Why hadn't he called?

"It won't ring because you scowl at it." Lizzie was curled up in the corner of the sagging blue sofa filing her nails. The usually overflowing mobile home was blessedly quiet since the rest of the brood had gone to play at the home of some friends, and their mother was taking a nap.

Wishing she weren't so transparent, Jennifer tucked a strand of her long blond hair behind her ear and opened her book again. "I don't know what you're talking about."

"You can call *him*."

"I already left a message. He's a grown man. If he can't be bothered to keep his promises, I'm not going to hound him."

"Poor Jennifer. You're head over heels for the guy."

"Even if I were head over heels—which I'm not—Avery and I had a deal. If he backs out, I'm not going to beg."

"So he dropped you like a hot rock, again."

"This isn't about personal feelings. This is about honoring a commitment." Jennifer slammed her book shut, making Lizzie look up in alarm.

Jennifer drew up her knees and rested her chin on them. "The man is a player. I don't know why I expected better from him this time."

She thought they shared something special together on their ride yesterday. He had opened up in a way he had never done before. She had started caring about him all over again.

No. That wasn't true. She had never stopped caring about him.

Dejected, Jennifer left her place at the dining

room table and crossed the room to plop down beside her sister. Lizzie slipped her arm across Jennifer's shoulders and pulled her close. Appreciating the comforting hug, Jennifer allowed herself a moment of self-pity. "Why couldn't he be dependable instead of charming?"

"Want me to call him and give him a piece of my mind?"

Mustering a grin, Jennifer said, "As kind as the offer is, you don't have much mind left to spare. You'd better hold on to what little you have."

"Ha! Ha!" Pulling her arm away from Jennifer's shoulder, Lizzie used it to elbow her sister in the ribs.

"Hey, that hurt."

"Serves you right for moping over a guy."

"Oh, like you weren't moping over Dale Marcus last week."

"Okay, maybe I was, but I learned my lesson and so should you. As Mom always says, there are plenty of fish in the sea. Now, show a little backbone and forget about him."

Rising from the sofa, Jennifer fisted her hands on her hips. "You're right. I won't give Avery Barnes another thought. If he can't see what a pearl I am then who needs him? Except…I need him to teach me how to handle a sword or I'm going to make a fool of myself in front of a lot of people."

"Maybe Mom can teach you the rest."

"She needs to stay off her leg."

The phone rang suddenly. Before Jennifer could dash over to answer it, Lizzie grabbed her by the arm. "Let the machine pick up. You don't want to sound like you have nothing to do except wait for him to call."

The second and third ring sent hope rising in Jennifer's heart, but she decided her sister was right. The fourth and fifth rings were almost more than she could stand.

The click of the answering machine coming on was followed by their mother's voice instructing the caller to leave a message after the beep. A shaky male voice said, "Yeah, hey, this is Dale Marcus…ah, could Lizzie…like… call me back?"

With a squeal of delight, Lizzie sprang up from the sofa and grabbed the receiver.

Jennifer walked to the table and picked up her book. A small thread of worry began to unspool in her mind. Why hadn't Avery come by? Why hadn't he called?

Lizzie covered the phone with one hand and turned to Jennifer. "Can I go watch Dale and his band practice for a little while? They're playing at the church youth center tonight. Pastor McGregor will be there and so will a couple of my girlfriends, and their parents. Please?"

At least one of them should be able to enjoy the evening. "Sure. I'll drive you into town. It's not like I'm doing anything else."

"Great. You're the best, Jen."

"I know, I know. God blessed you from birth with me as your big sister."

"It's true." She pulled her hand from the phone. "I'll see you in a few minutes, Dale. Thanks for inviting me."

Jennifer gathered her truck keys from the hook on the wall and checked in on her mother. Mary was sitting propped up in bed reading her Bible. Jennifer put the cordless phone on her bedside table. "I'm going to run Lizzie into town. Do you need anything?"

Mary closed her book. "No. I'm fine. I'm going to catch up on a little more reading and then try a nap. One good thing has come out of this fiasco. I'm not using my busy life as an excuse to avoid reading the Good Book. I needed this time with God."

"He does move in mysterious ways."

"Yes. Who would expect Him to use a rabbit to get me back in the habit of prayer-ful contemplation?"

"He must really like Isabella. He's used her to change a lot of lives. I've got my cell phone and I'll be back in twenty minutes. Are you sure you don't need anything?"

"If you happen to stop at the Get-N-Go, we need some milk and would you bring me a bag of red licorice?"

"Sure. Was it a favorite of Henrietta Dutton?"

"I have no idea, but it's a favorite of mine. Thanks, honey. Be careful."

After they left the house, it took less than ten minutes to reach the church and drop off Lizzie. Turning back out onto the highway, Jennifer drove another half dozen blocks to the convenience store.

Pulling up, she parked at the side of the building and went in. After picking up a package of the candy her mother wanted, she walked back to the coolers at the rear of the store and pulled a gallon of milk from the rack.

Standing in front of the freezer section, she was debating the cost in unwanted pounds versus the comfort a carton of chocolate silk ice cream might provide when the bell over the door jingled announcing another costumer. The sound was followed by a loud giggle. Jennifer glanced over her shoulder and saw Avery enter.

He wasn't alone. A stunning redhead had her

hands clasped around his arm. Standing on tiptoe, she planted a kiss on his cheek and giggled again at something he said. Smiling, Avery happened to glance toward the back of the store and his gaze collided with Jennifer's.

She quickly turned back to stare at the freezer door.

He isn't working late. He hasn't wrecked his car. He has a hot date. I can't believe I spent the last two hours worrying about the man.

Calling herself every kind of fool, Jennifer stood with her head bowed for a few long minutes. Finally, she pulled two cartons of ice cream from the freezer and marched toward the counter at the front. Avery had already paid for his purchases and left. She was treated to the sight of him pulling out onto the highway with Ms. Giggles snuggled close to his side.

Chapter Eleven

Gravel flew out from beneath his tires as Avery stepped on the accelerator and tore out of the parking lot. He was trying to forget the sight of Jennifer standing at the back of the convenience store. He knew she had seen him. The hurt in her eyes left a hollow feeling in the pit of his stomach.

"I love your car." The woman seated beside him rubbed a hand over the rich leather upholstery.

"Thanks. So do I."

Was her name Bitsy or Betsy? He couldn't be sure. She had been part of a group taking a tour of the stables and museum at the fort earlier that afternoon. It had been obvious from the start that she had little interest in the history lessons being presented. When the group moved on, she had stayed behind, admiring his car. His offer to take her for a spin in it had been met with giggles of delight.

"How do you afford a car like this on army pay?"

He glanced over and caught the speculative gleam in her eyes. "Family money."

"Really?" Her eyes brightened. "It must be nice. Unless, of course, it's your wife's money."

"No, no wife."

"That's even better. Where are we going?"

Where *was* he going? He was racing headlong down the highway without a destination, without a clue. The woman beside him was a stranger. The woman he wanted beside him was back in the Get-N-Go with a gallon of milk in her hands and eyes filled with disappointment.

He hadn't planned on running into Jennifer. Since his confrontation with his grandfather, he'd just felt like running. Away from responsibility—away from his own insecurities. He'd spent years perfecting the art of being less than what his grandfather expected. A pretty stranger, a fast car and reckless behavior had usually been his answer.

Until now. Until Jennifer.

She wasn't running from her responsibilities or her insecurities. She faced her problems head-on. Where did she find the courage?

The answer was simple. All he had to do was look at the way she lived her life. With faith.

He'd let her down, broken his promises. His grandfather didn't get to witness his stupid performance today—Jennifer did.

Forcing the troubling thoughts to the back of his mind, he glanced at the woman beside him. "Where do you want to go?"

She threw her hand in the air. "Someplace fun. Someplace exciting. Surprise me."

Surprise her. Surprise yourself. Do the right thing for once.

He took his foot off the gas and the car's speed dropped as he contemplated his options. The knot in his stomach eased as he realized he had already made up his mind.

He said, "I'm afraid this is as far as I can go."

"What? Oh, don't say that. We're just getting started. Kansas City is only two hours from here. We can see the sights and try out the nightlife."

When his car slowed enough, he made a U-turn and started back toward the post. "Sorry. I've got to get back to my duties."

"What a bummer." She scooted away from him. "I thought we were going to have some fun."

"The U.S. Army is very strict when it comes to a soldier doing his duty."

"I suppose. It was sweet of you to take me for a ride. I've never been in a Jaguar before."

"It's just four wheels and an engine."

"That is *so* not true."

"Where can I drop you off? I think your tour may be finished at the cavalry museum by now."

She gave him the name of a local motel and he pressed the gas once more, suddenly in a hurry to drop her off. And as odd as it seemed, he felt right about doing it. It was the best decision he had made in months.

An hour later, he knocked at the Grants' front door. Toby opened it, scowling at him. "What do you want?"

"Is Jennifer home?"

"Nope."

Avery reined in his disappointment. "Where is she?"

"Studying."

"At the campus library?" He took a step backward, eager to find her and explain. To tell her he was sorry. To make it up to her somehow.

"Nope." Toby's short reply stopped Avery in his tracks.

"Where is she studying?"

"At a friend's."

Avery could tell by the look in the teen's eyes that he wasn't going to get any more information, but he tried anyway. "I know I messed up. Would you please tell me where I can find her?"

"Nope."

Admitting defeat at the hands of a boy half his age wasn't easy, but Avery knew when to give in. "Would you at least tell her that I stopped by?"

"Sure. If I don't forget." Toby closed the door and snapped off the porch light, leaving Avery standing alone in the dark.

The next afternoon, at twenty minutes after four, Avery drove up to Jennifer's home. She was standing on the front porch, sweeping the steps. She glanced up once, then returned to swinging the broom with renewed vigor.

She looked mad.

He stepped out of the car with a pair of sabers in his hand and waited for her to say something, anything. She just kept sweeping.

He deserved her anger, but the silent treatment wasn't what he had expected. Jennifer wasn't normally at a loss for words.

Deciding that if she didn't mention yesterday, neither would he, he walked up to her and handed her one of the swords he carried. "I thought today we'd go over some hand-to-hand combat moves."

"All right." She set the broom aside and took the scabbard he held out to her.

Pulling the sword from its cover, she turned and walked to a clear space in the yard. "Is this where I get to say *en garde?*"

She spun around with the blade extended. Only his quick reflexes allowed him to block her weapon with his own, saving him from a nasty bruise on his arm.

"Will you be careful!"

Her eyes widened and she pressed a hand to her mouth. "Oh, I'm so sorry," she said, her voice thick with disdain.

She took a step back, but the glint in her eyes looked anything but apologetic. Holding her free hand aloft, she extended the point toward him while rocking back and forth on the balls of her feet.

"I thrust like this, right?" She lunged toward him but he struck her blade aside.

"Jennifer, this is serious. You could hurt someone."

Her eyes narrowed as if considering her options. "They aren't sharp. I can't actually cut you—or stab you—or slice you into ribbons."

Extending her blade again, she made tiny circling motions in front of his chest.

Grasping the end of her saber, he forced it down. "If this is about yesterday, I can explain."

Jerking her weapon out of his grasp, she retreated a pace and held it up again. "I saw you with the explanation. She had red hair and she was draped over your arm like a wet horse blanket."

"I thought we wouldn't let this get personal."

"Oh, it's personal, but don't think it's about who you were with. You can date every woman on the planet as far as I'm concerned."

"Then why are you so mad?"

"Because I'm serious about taking my mother's place in the festival. I gave my word that I would do it and I *will* do it to the best of my ability and *you* said you would help me."

"So I took a day off."

"You couldn't call and tell me you couldn't make it? No. You let me worry that something had happened to you."

He tipped his head to the side. "You were worried about me?"

"Yes—no. That's not the point. The point is that you are selfish and self-centered and you don't care about anyone."

"That's true."

"Oh, yes it is!" she shot back automatically.

He held up his hands up in surrender. "I'm agreeing with you, Jennifer."

Her eyebrows shot up. "You are?"

He nodded. "I'm selfish. I'm self-centered. I'm the scum of the earth. I agreed to teach you and I failed to live up to my side of the bargain. Blowing you off yesterday was totally inexcusable."

Clearly puzzled, she lowered her blade. "Yes, it was."

"I'm sorry I worried you by not calling."

Her eyes narrowed and she whipped the sword up, pointing it at his midsection. "You sound contrite, but I'm not buying it."

"I am contrite. I won't miss another day. I'll put it in writing if you want me to."

"You should write 'I'm sorry' one hundred times in your notebook. That's what Mrs. Craig makes me do. Are you going to stab him, sis?" Ryan stood by with Isabella clutched in his arms. The rabbit's eyes were wide. Her nose twitched and her whiskers quivered with excitement. She looked eager to join the battle.

Jennifer lowered her sword, embarrassed and ashamed to be caught menacing Avery. She was usually careful not to lose her temper when her younger siblings were within hearing distance. "I'm not going to stab anyone, Ryan."

"Thank goodness," Avery mumbled.

She ignored him and smiled at her brother. "Avery and I are just…"

"Pretending to be fighting," Avery supplied.

She cast him a grateful look, then scowled. She

didn't want to be grateful to him for any reason. Turning her attention back to Ryan, she said, "You shouldn't have Isabella out of the barn."

"But she's tired of being inside. She wants to run around," Ryan insisted.

Jennifer walked to Ryan and dropped to her knees. "We don't have a safe place for her to play. You wouldn't want her to get loose and get hurt, would you?"

"No. I guess not."

"Come on, sport," Avery said. "I'll go with you. Once she's back in her hutch I have something to show you."

Ryan's eyes brightened. "What?"

"You'll see. Let's be responsible first and make sure Isabella is safe. Okay?"

"Okey-dokey."

Jennifer didn't snort at Avery's comment, but she felt like it. He certainly wasn't a poster child for responsibility. When the pair disappeared into the barn, she blew out a deep breath.

Avery had shown his true colors once again. Looking at the weapon in her hand, she sliced it through the air in a wide arc. Any infatuation for him that had been lingering was gone now. She had herself and her emotions well in hand.

Sliding the saber back into its scabbard, she congratulated herself on facing him like the mature woman she was. When he and Ryan came out of the barn, Avery had his hand on one of the boy's shoulders and the two of them were grinning at each other.

So what if he looked handsome and relaxed? It didn't matter.

He and Ryan walked to the rear of Avery's car. From inside the trunk, Avery pulled out a bicycle and set it on the ground in front of Ryan. Her brother's shout of joy startled her as he grabbed the handlebars and straddled the frame.

Ryan quickly peddled around the yard as he yelled, "Look Jennifer, Avery got my bike fixed! Can I go to Nate's house? Please?"

Avery might be able to charm her little brother into thinking he was something special, but it wouldn't work on her.

When had Avery taken Ryan's bike to get it repaired?

Ryan raced toward her and skidded to a stop a few feet away. "It's as good as new. Can I go to Nate's house?"

His friend Nate lived in the next farmhouse a quarter mile down the road.

"When did Avery take your bike, Ryan?"

"The first day he came to see you. I'm paying him for getting it fixed. That's okay, isn't it?"

"How are you paying him?"

"By polishing his car wheels. I'm going to do it every week that he's here. I've been doing a good job. Avery said so."

"I'm sure you have, sweetheart."

"Can I go to Nate's?"

"All right, but be back before six. It starts getting dark earlier now."

"Okay, thanks." He pushed off, peddling furiously along the edge of the drive.

Turning to look at Avery, she saw he wasn't paying any attention to her. He was pulling a burlap padded target from his trunk.

She closed the distance between, annoyed that he had managed to make her like him a little once more. "You didn't have to fix Ryan's bike. I would have taken care of it before long."

"A guy needs his wheels. Besides, it isn't like I slaved over a hot forge to fix it. A couple of guys at the motor pool did it as a favor."

"Be sure and thank them for us."

"I will. Are you ready for today's lesson?"

"I was ready yesterday." Her remark sounded childish and she regretted it instantly.

"Yeah. I already said I was sorry."

"I only have a week left to learn this stuff. If you aren't going to help me then say so and let me find someone else."

"Jennifer, in spite of what you might think,

I'm as serious as you are. Captain Watson, the army brass, they want this win. I want to give it to them."

"Okay then." She resolved to let the matter drop, even though she still didn't trust his commitment. "We will meet here every day next week at four-thirty sharp, ready to work."

He nodded. "We'll also need to meet on the field where you're making your ride as soon as possible."

"I guess that's true. Okay."

"Do you have a pistol?"

"Yes, my mother has one at the Dutton mansion. How soon will I need it?"

"A couple of days, depending on how you do with the saber. Will we be able to shoot here?"

"Yes. Unless the neighbors complain."

"We'll use a small charge of powder to start with. It shouldn't bother anyone. You'll need to learn how to handle a gun on foot before you learn how to shoot from horseback."

"That makes sense."

"Good. Today, I've brought a target so you can start practicing saber hits. Is there someplace we can hang this up?"

Jennifer buckled the sword around her waist and shifted it to the proper position. "Inside the barn would be best."

Leading the way, she helped him hoist and tie up the burlap dummy. He was all business the rest of the afternoon. Part of her wanted to find fault with his manner—she wasn't quite ready to forgive him—but he remained professional and courteous as he demonstrated how to make the slashing strokes the saber had been designed for.

Besides, it was hard not to admire someone who could wield a sword with such ease and manage to look like a swashbuckling hero straight out of a movie at the same time.

He taught her how to hit targets on both her left and her right sides. It was hard and tiring work, but under his guidance, it wasn't long before she was doing a little swashbuckling herself.

While her skill level rose throughout the afternoon, her determination to remain detached and cool to Avery faded. His smiles and encouraging words weren't flirtatious or deriding for a change, but carried what seemed like genuine warmth. If she hadn't seen him with another woman yesterday, she might have thought he had some affection for her.

Giving herself a mental shake, she decided not to go there and struck the burlap dummy with renewed vigor.

When their lesson was finished and Avery left, she waited until his car was out of sight before she let down her guard and examined the feelings crowding into her mind.

She flexed her sore arm. It was no use. Hitting the dummy hadn't helped. She still cared for Avery, and she didn't know how to change those feelings.

Chapter Twelve

Avery was ten minutes early again the next afternoon. He had traded his sports car for one of the unit's red pickups and matching horse trailers. As he stepped out of the truck, he realized just how eager he was to see Jennifer again.

He didn't bother trying to hide the truth from himself. He was falling for her—hard and fast.

Glancing at the house, he saw Toby waiting on the front porch. The boy stood and walked toward Avery. He stopped a few feet away, crossed his arms over his chest and fixed his gaze on the ground.

"Thanks for getting squirt's bike fixed." It was apparent Toby had a hard time getting the words out.

Avery knew the boy didn't want to be

beholden to him for anything. "It was the least I could do. Where is Jennifer?"

"She took Mom to one of her historical society meetings. She'll be back in a few minutes."

Gesturing toward the truck bed, Avery asked, "Can you give me a hand with this stuff?"

"What is it?"

"A couple of dummies my unit uses for practice. Your sister is ready to start working from horseback. I want to set these up in the corral."

"Why does your outfit ride horses anyway? It's lame."

Avery took a moment to answer. "You think the army should only be about guns and tanks?"

"I watch the news. You and your buddies aren't riding horses into battle against terrorists. How did you get such a cushy assignment, anyway?"

Avery had heard the question from a lot of visitors to the unit. "Soldiers are assigned to the Commanding General's Mounted Color Guard from various units already stationed at Fort Riley. They do ask for volunteers, but I wasn't one of them. I liked the idea of being inside a tank. I'm attached to one of the armored divisions, on loan to the CGMCG for eighteen months."

"So you didn't have a choice?"

"Not really, but once I realized what the

mounted guard is all about, I was proud to be chosen."

"So what is it about?"

"It's about tradition and keeping the spirit of the past alive. I'll bet you think of cavalry troops in the old west as crack shots and daring horsemen."

"Sure. They had to be."

"No. The truth is most of them were boys not much older than you are from cities and small towns and farms. Few of them had ever fired a gun, some had never ridden a horse before they enlisted, almost none of them owned a saber or knew how to use one."

"Are you sure about that?"

"Think of today's army. How many men have driven tanks or fired missiles before they joined up?"

"Not many."

"A well-trained cavalry was the cutting edge of military tactics a hundred and fifty years ago, the same way laser-guided shells are now. Soldiers in my unit are trained using the same manuals that were used in the Civil War. I'm proud to be a part of that tradition. If that inspires another man to join up and serve his country, then I've done my job."

"Now you sound like my mother."

"I draw the line at putting on a corset to recruit anyone."

That coaxed a ghost of a smile from the boy. "After you've done your time in the color guard, will you go back to your old unit?"

"I will. I'll have two more years to serve before my enlistment is up."

"So, you could be sent to a war zone."

"That's possible."

"Would you go?"

"Yes."

"Would you fight?"

It wasn't the first time Avery had thought about the question, but it was the first time the answer came to him so readily. "Yes."

"Wouldn't you be scared?"

"Yes, I would be scared, but I hope I would do my job. I don't think a man can ever truly know if he will be a coward until he faces that moment, but I know that this country, and what we stand for, is worth fighting for."

Toby regarded him without saying anything else. The sound of Jennifer's truck rolling down the driveway made them both look up. Toby reached into the bed of Avery's truck and pulled out part of the target. "Where do you want this?"

"The center of the corral should be fine."

"I doubt she'll be able to hit it."

"If she doesn't, then I'm a poor teacher."

"You're getting better. At least this time you showed up."

Jennifer stopped the truck beside Avery's and paused to gather her composure. All during church that morning she had prayed for the strength to keep her emotions under control. She was determined to be calm and cool.

If only she would keep her rebellious heart from beating faster at the sight of him.

Ryan jumped out almost as soon as the vehicle rolled to a stop and raced to help his new idol lift something out of the back of his pickup. Jennifer didn't know how to curb Ryan's new hero worship. She wasn't even sure she should try. She certainly wasn't having any success stopping the growth of her own emotional attachment to Avery.

Getting out of her vehicle, she nodded toward him. "What's all this?"

"Your targets. We'll have them set up in a few minutes. Would you mind not wearing one of those skirts this evening?"

She laid a finger against her cheek and tapped it as she considered his request. "Let me see. Look like a fool in a long skirt or look normal in jeans? Decisions, decisions."

"You don't look foolish in the dresses. I'm just concerned about safety. If you're unhorsed, I don't want you getting tangled up in all that material."

Her eyebrows shot up. "Unhorsed? You think I might fall off my horse?"

She couldn't help but feel insulted by his suggestion. They both knew she was a much better rider than he was.

A wary expression settled over his features. Slowly, he said, "In the *extremely* unlikely event…that such a…*freak* accident should occur, I'd rather you were wearing pants."

Mollified slightly, she nodded. "In that case, I'll do as you suggest."

"Good." He relaxed and turned toward the corral with a metal pole and stand in his hands.

She followed him and watched as he and Toby set up two targets. Each tall metal pole had a cross arm that extended out about three feet. A stuffed burlap bag with large red and white circles painted on it hung from the arm about five feet off the ground. As they finished, she saddled Lollypop and rode into the arena.

Avery came to stand beside her and handed her a saber. His hand rested briefly on her knee as he stared up at her. "No funny stuff, no showing off, Jennifer. This is serious. The blade isn't sharp but you can hurt your horse or yourself if you aren't careful."

She took the sword and rested it across the pommel of her saddle. "I'll do exactly as you say."

"Good. Walk Lollypop past both targets and hit them with the slicing motion I showed you yesterday. Keep close to the targets. Don't try to reach for them. You'll unbalance yourself and your horse. That's where ninety percent of riders make their mistakes."

"Okay. I've got it. How hard can it be?"

Nudging Lollypop forward, she rode past the dummy and sliced the blade sideways. It struck the target with a satisfying thud, but the weight of the blade carried it downward and it bounced into Lollypop's flank making the mare sidestep.

"Oh, sorry, baby, sorry," Jennifer crooned to the horse.

Adjusting her grip on the hilt of the saber, she raised it over Lollypop's neck and swung at the target on the opposite side. This time she controlled the blade's descent. It took more arm strength than she expected. It also took her concentration off the horse and Lollypop swerved to the left as Jennifer's weight shifted.

"Not bad," Avery called from the other end of the corral. "Circle back and do it twice more then progress to a trot. Shift your weight more forward in the saddle."

She did as he asked and made two more passes at a walk, then advanced to a trot without any difficulty. Proud of herself, she rode back and stopped in front of Avery. "What do you think?"

"You've got a good seat. You still lack some upper body strength, but you can work on that."

Hoping for a little more praise, she resisted making a snappy comeback. "I want to try it at a gallop."

"I think you should stick to the trot for a little longer."

"No, I can do it from a gallop."

"Okay, if you think you're ready." He stepped back.

When Jennifer kicked Lollypop, the little mare responded by zipping toward the first dummy. Leaning forward, Jennifer extended her arm. She didn't have time to slash downward and ended up stabbing the burlap as she shot past. The blade stayed imbedded in the dummy and yanked out of her hand.

Pulling her horse to a stop, Jennifer whirled around to glare at Avery. If he laughed!

He had one arm crossed over his chest and his other hand covering his jaw. He turned his back to her and took several steps away before turning back. Ryan and Toby, watching from outside the fence, both doubled up with mirth.

Trotting Lollypop back to the target, Jennifer grasped the sword and pulled it free.

Avery waved his hand in a circle. "Try it again."

She heard the amusement brimming in his tone. "If you laugh, so help me…"

He threw both hands up in surrender. "Not laughing. No laughing here."

Ryan fell to the ground in a fit of giggles and Toby sputtered a few times, but recovered himself when she glared at him.

"It's not as easy as it looks," she told them.

"I believe you," Toby managed to say before another guffaw escaped him.

"You work on it a few more times," Avery said, "I'm going to saddle Dakota."

Ignoring her brothers, she focused on galloping past one target and timing her strikes. By the fifth pass, she felt she had the hang of it. Setting Lollypop into a sixth run, Jennifer tried striking both targets. She missed the second one completely and managed to whack her own knee in the process.

She threw the saber to the ground in a fit of temper and rubbed her leg.

Avery rode up beside her. "That will leave a bruise."

She closed her eyes. "This is the most idiotic thing I've ever tried to do. I'm going to look like a moron in front of the entire town and all the visitors and dignitaries, not to mention the famous Dutton descendants. Why did I ever agree to do this?"

"Because you love your mother."

She glared at him from beneath lowered lashes. "Not as much as I did an hour ago."

He chuckled. "You'll get the hang of it. You're not as bad as some of the recruits I've trained lately."

She straightened in the saddle. "Really?"

"No. You're the worst I've ever seen."

Mouth agape, she sputtered, "I am not. Am I?"

"Will you relax? Don't think of this as a military exercise. Think of it as fun."

Ryan had crawled between the fence rails and ran to pick up her sword. He brought it to her and held it up. "You're doing great, sis. You didn't fall off once."

"Thanks, Ryan. Do you want to ride Lollypop while Avery puts Dakota through his paces? I'm done."

She stepped down and hoisted her brother into the saddle in her place, then turned and held the saber out, hilt first, toward Avery. "Why don't you show us how it's done."

Taking the weapon, he held the blade straight in front of his face in a salute. "Yes, ma'am."

Wheeling Dakota, he charged down the corral and effortlessly slashed both targets hard enough to send them spinning. Pulling his mount to a sliding stop, he spun his horse and charged again, striking both dummies before coming to a sliding stop beside Jennifer.

She looked up at Ryan. His eyes were as round as silver dollars. He said, "That was awesome, dude."

Grinning, Jennifer patted her brother's knee. "That's how I'll look when I'm doing great."

"I'm gonna do that someday." He kicked Lollypop into motion and rode around past the targets stabbing them with an imaginary sword.

Jennifer turned to Avery. "I went online and downloaded the required moves that the judges will be looking for in your military horsemanship."

"Great. Were do we start?"

"According to the guidelines, you'll enter dismounted, walk to a predetermined starting point and halt. Then you'll mount and salute. They'll be looking for correct leading and leading on a straight line, correct mounting and they'll also be looking for at your horse's calmness."

"A jittery trooper makes a jittery mount?"

"Something like that."

He dismounted and walked beside her to the corral gate. He wasn't particularly tall, but she felt dainty beside him. The small brass spurs on his boots jingled faintly with each step he took. She caught a whiff of his aftershave. He smelled like expensive leather, warm spices and soft woods. A quiver settled in the pit of her stomach and left her smiling softly. There was so much she liked about him. If only she could put her trust in him. If only *he* could learn to put his trust in God.

When they reached the fence, he paused and looked down at her. "Tell me what I'm doing wrong and I'll do better."

She blinked twice. "What?"

"With my horsemanship."

"Oh, right." She wanted to smack her own forehead. Of course he hadn't been talking about their relationship. They didn't have a relationship so how could he be thinking along those lines? Certainly, they had shared a few dates in the past and he had even kissed her then—recalling those brief moments of happiness warmed her to her toes—but since then he'd made it clear that a relationship with her was the *last* thing he wanted.

He tipped his head to the side. "Are you all right?"

Trying for indifference, she replied, "Yes. Why do you ask?"

He leaned closer. "Your face is flushed."

She pressed her hands to her traitorous cheeks. "It is? How odd. It must be all this exercise."

"Shall I start?"

Extending her arm, she motioned for him to proceed. "Yes, go on." *Before I kiss you.*

Chapter Thirteen

For one horrible second Jennifer thought she had spoken aloud, but Avery walked away with Dakota without a backward look.

"Thank you, dear Lord, for small favors," she whispered.

The last thing she wanted was for Avery to discover just how much she cared for him.

This was business. She needed to keep it professional. He needed her help to win the Sheridan Cup. He wasn't interested in rekindling old fires. Was he?

Of course not, and neither was she.

Once she had her mind back on the task at hand, she was able to settle into her coaching mode.

"Ask him to lengthen his stride," she called

out, wanting to see Dakota move forward with longer steps.

Immediately Avery tensed. Knowing a horse could sense mental or physical tension, she wasn't surprised when Dakota's trot became choppy instead of smoother.

"Stop a minute," she called out and walked up to them. She laid a hand on Dakota's neck and stroked him as she looked up at Avery.

Avery let out a frustrated breath. "Tell me what I did wrong."

"You forgot to smile."

"Don't try to be kind. I could feel it wasn't right."

"That's because you know Dakota so well."

"He and I have spent a lot of hours together since Lindsey left the unit. What were we doing wrong?"

"You were thinking too hard."

He relaxed and gave her a half smile. "This is supposed to fun, right?"

"Yup. Who cares what score you get? Riding a horse is *fun.* Can you remember that?"

"I think so."

"Good. Try it again with a smile. Just a little one."

Avery took her suggestions and relaxed as he put Dakota through his paces. The improvement was impressive. While he'd had some trouble communicating with McCloud, he and Dakota were obviously on the same wavelength. Before long, they were operating as a responsive and intuitive team.

Jennifer relaxed, too, and began to enjoy watching them work together.

It was almost dark by the time Jennifer called a halt to the lessons for the evening. Avery couldn't help the pang of disappointment that followed her words. He didn't want the session to end. He didn't want to go home to his empty apartment.

"What do you say to a quick gallop?" he suggested as she held open the gate for him.

"I can't." He heard the longing in her voice, but saw the resolve settle over her face.

"I need to pick up my mother and Lizzie, and then I really need to crack the books. I have a paper due tomorrow."

"Okay." Dismounting, he loosened the girth on Dakota's saddle. He wanted to tease and cajole her into going with him, but he didn't press the issue. Being sensitive to what she needed was harder than he thought. He was used to only thinking about himself.

"I'll take a rain check," she offered as they began walking toward his truck and trailer.

"I'll hold you to that."

Not tonight, but soon, when she wasn't pressed for time or swamped with responsibilities. Once her re-enactment and his competition were over, they might be able to spend a leisurely afternoon together on a trail ride. He knew of a bridle path that meandered along the shore of a local lake. His heart lightened at the thought of spending time there alone with her.

"What's your plan for tomorrow?" she asked.

"Pistols."

She arched her brows. "Really? Am I ready for that?"

"I think so."

Suddenly, Dakota whinnied loudly and began to pull at the reins.

"Easy, boy." Avery patted the big bay's neck to calm him, but Dakota whinnied again. Avery and Jennifer exchanged puzzled looks as the horse stood with his head high and his gaze fastened on the barn door.

Jennifer began to laugh. "He smells Isabella."

Shaking his head in disbelief, Avery allowed the horse to pull him to the barn door. Dakota stretched his head and neck in as far as he could over the lower half of the door and whinnied softly this time.

Jennifer motioned to Ryan. "Get Isabella out of her cage, honey. Dakota wants to see her."

Avery made Dakota back up enough to allow Ryan to slip inside and open the rabbit's hutch. Before he could lift Isabella out, she hopped down and darted to the door. She hopped up and down madly, until Dakota lowered his nose to hers.

As the odd couple nuzzled each other, Avery glanced down at Jennifer standing beside him. "You're right. She is what he wanted."

"It must be love," she noted softly, and glanced up at him.

Their eyes met and held. Her pupils darkened, some deep emotion stirring in their depths. He wanted to reach out and cup her cheek with his hand, but he held back, suddenly afraid that he might destroy what he saw.

"I think they're just good friends," Ryan remarked as he knelt beside Isabella and stroked Dakota's forehead.

Toby, standing a few feet away, said dryly, "Of course they're just friends. They couldn't be anything else."

Jennifer looked away. A blush stained her cheeks bright pink. "I should get going. I don't want to keep Mom and Lizzie waiting."

Reaching out, Avery caught her hand before she turned away. "Why don't you let me pick them up? That way you can get a head start on the studying you have to do."

She shook her head. "Thanks for the offer but it isn't necessary. I can manage."

He leaned closer. "Still won't admit that you can't do it all?"

Rolling her eyes, she said, "I knew I was going to regret telling you that."

"Give me the keys to your truck," he coaxed. "I'll leave Dakota to visit with his bunny friend for a while longer and go pick up your mother and sister."

She bit her lip. He could see her wavering.

Quickly, he added, "Unlike you, I don't have anything else to do tonight."

She seemed to notice that he was still holding her hand. She withdrew it slowly. "I could use the extra time for some online research."

"Great. Where are your keys?" He hated letting go of her, but tried not to show it.

"They're in the truck. Are you sure you don't mind?"

"Friends help out friends. Right? And no, I don't mind at all." He turned to Ryan. "Grab hold of Hippy Hoppy."

When Ryan had Isabella securely in his arms,

Avery opened the barn door and led Dakota inside. Pulling the saddle and bridle off, he carried them back outside and closed the door. Dakota lowered his nose to the straw, turned around twice and then lay down. Ryan put Isabella down and she immediately hopped over to her friend.

Avery looked at Jennifer. "What are you still doing out here? Go study."

She grinned. "Thank you. I may actually get my paper done before midnight."

"Not if you stand here talking."

"I'll call Mom and let her know you are on your way." Saluting, she turned and hurried to the house, pausing to look back and wave before she went in.

Happy that he could lighten a small part of the burdens she shouldered, he laid his saddle in the back of his truck and crossed to her vehicle. The keys were in the ignition. Getting in, he started the engine. Before he put it in gear, he noticed a small silver cross dangling from the rearview mirror. Reaching up, he cupped the smooth metal and smiled.

Jennifer took her faith with her wherever she went and she wasn't afraid to display it for everyone to see.

A sharp rap on the window drew his attention. Toby motioned for him to roll down the window. The boy was having a hard time keeping a grin off his face. "It was nice of you to give my sister a break, but don't you think you should ask where my mother is?"

Avery laughed at himself. "I'm sure that would have occurred to me in a minute or two."

"She and the nut cluster are meeting at the Dutton Inn. You can't miss it. There's a big sign out front that says Historical Bed and Breakfast. How lame is that? Like breakfast is a historical meal."

Thankful for Toby's help, Avery rolled up the window and drove off.

On the way into town, his mind kept wandering back to the expression he had seen in Jennifer's eyes.

"It must be love," he repeated to himself, half afraid to say the words out loud.

Had Jennifer been talking about something other than the rabbit's affections? Was it possible she had been talking about her own feelings?

He hadn't given her a reason to care for him. In fact, he had gone out of his way to do just the opposite up until the day before yesterday.

Still, she hadn't kicked him off her property. She might claim it was because of the commitment she'd made but something told him there was more to it. Perhaps he hadn't damaged their relationship beyond repair. If she gave him enough time, could he prove he was worthy of her affections?

A faint hope began to grow in his heart. He glanced at the cross on the mirror. "If I was a praying man, I'd be asking for Your help."

He smiled as he realized Jennifer would tell him that that was a prayer. And she would be right.

As Toby had promised, the bed and breakfast was clearly marked on the outskirts of town. By the number of people milling around on the wide green lawn, Avery surmised the meeting had just let out. He saw Mary Grant, leaning on her crutches, in animated conversation with several townspeople. Lizzie was sitting on a bench nearby.

A few of the crowd had already headed to their cars lining both sides of the street, and Avery was able to get a parking spot close to the front walk. Lizzie caught sight of him and waved, then headed toward him.

Avery got out and walked around to the passenger's side and opened the door. Lizzie walked past him and climbed in. "Am I glad to see you. This was so borrrring!"

"You're just upset because Dale wasn't here."

Mary's voice brimmed with humor. "I know you 'volunteered' to stay with me because you were hoping to see him. You can't fool your mother."

Avery hid a grin as Lizzie rolled her eyes. When he glanced toward Mary, he got a major shock. It wasn't a local man assisting her. His grandfather was walking with her toward the vehicle.

"Be careful of this sidewalk, Mrs. Grant, it's very uneven," Edmond cautioned, keeping a close eye on her halting steps.

"I'm fine, sir, but thank you for your concern."

"Please, you must call me Edmond." He smiled when she cast a shy look in his direction.

"If you will call me Mary."

"I'd be delighted to do so." Edmond looked up and stopped in his tracks when he caught sight of Avery.

Struggling to hide his anger, Avery fumed silently. The old man might look surprised to see him, but Avery didn't buy it. Edmond always had a plan. That he would use Jennifer's family in his attempt to worm his way back into Avery's good graces was a new low—even for Edmond.

Avery inclined his head slightly. "Grandfather. I didn't know you were a history buff."

Edmond recovered quickly. "Neither did I, but Mrs. Grant is showing me the error of my ways."

Mary blushed like a schoolgirl as she handed Avery her crutches and slid in beside Lizzie. "Your poor grandfather was sitting in the parlor reading and I'm afraid we swooped in and surrounded him. We simply take over the inn when we get together."

"That's true," Lizzie muttered.

"I enjoyed myself, Mary," Edmond assured her. "I look forward to watching your granddaughter in the re-enactment of Henrietta Dutton's ride next week. It sounds thrilling."

Avery scowled at him. "You're staying to watch Jennifer's ride? I'm surprised you can be away from the firm for so long."

Mary beamed at Avery as she took her crutches from him. "Edmond isn't staying just for our festival. He's decided to stay until after the cavalry competition. I can't believe you didn't tell him that you're competing."

Chapter Fourteen

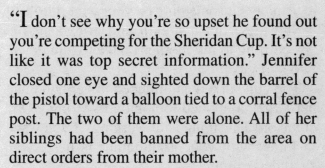

"I don't see why you're so upset he found out you're competing for the Sheridan Cup. It's not like it was top secret information." Jennifer closed one eye and sighted down the barrel of the pistol toward a balloon tied to a corral fence post. The two of them were alone. All of her siblings had been banned from the area on direct orders from their mother.

"I shouldn't have said anything to you." Avery regretted mentioning his feelings on the subject almost as soon as the words were out of his mouth.

"No. I'm glad you did. I know you and your grandfather haven't gotten along in the past, but maybe he has changed."

She fired. The balloon continued to wave in

the wind. She looked down at her smoking firearm. "Are you sure this is loaded?"

"Aim a little higher and keep at least one eye open this time. He never came to so much as a soccer practice when I was growing up. Now he's spending a month in Dutton, Kansas, so he can be here to watch me ride. I don't get it. I'd like to know the real reason he's hanging around."

"I had one eye open," she insisted.

"Then you're in trouble. Are you sure you have to actually hit something on your wild ride?"

She blew out a breath and aimed again. "According to my mother I have to gun down two bad guys."

The gun barked and jumped in her hand but her target continued to bob on its string. "Oh, come on! This thing isn't working. If you want to know why your grandfather is here, you should ask him."

Avery took the gun from her and fired one-handed, shattering the balloon. "I don't want to talk to him. I know he's looking for some way to humiliate me."

Her mouth dropped open and she stuck her hands on her hips. "The first two were blanks, weren't they?"

"They're all blanks. There are no bullets. I

keep telling you it's the hot powder that pops the targets."

She took the gun back from him and walked down the fence to a second red balloon. "Why are you so sure your grandfather has an ulterior motive in staying here?"

"His track record for one thing."

She had raised the gun with both hands and was sighting down the wobbling barrel, but she lowered it and waited until Avery met her gaze. "What did he do that you can't forgive?"

He jerked his head toward the target. "Shoot."

"If I hit this one you'll tell me?"

"No."

Her eyes narrowed. "Yes, you will."

"Fine. Hit it and I'll share."

Turning sideways, she brought the gun up in a smooth motion with one hand and fired. The target exploded. Her eyes widened. "I did it!"

"Lucky accident."

"It doesn't matter. Share." She folded her arms and stood waiting like Ma Barker clutching a smoking revolver.

"I changed my mind."

"If you tell me why you're so angry at your grandfather, I'll tell you about the time I took off all my clothes and ran through the grocery store."

That was a picture he would have a hard time getting out of his mind. "Okay. You first."

She shook her head. "No. Me after."

He debated the wisdom of sharing his story, but found he wanted to tell her. He wanted to share more with her than he had ever thought possible to share with any woman. He wanted her compassion, her laughter, her worry and her tears. He wanted to be included in her life.

The starting point was this. He took her gun and began to reload it, afraid to watch her face. "After my parents died I got in with a really fast and stupid crowd. I did a lot of things that I'm not proud of now, but then I met a woman named Miranda. She was so pretty and different. She came from a very poor family but that didn't matter to me. She worshiped the ground I walked on, or so I thought."

Jennifer took a step closer. "What happened?" she asked softly.

"I asked her to marry me. We planned a big wedding. I invited all my so-called friends. The marriage of Edmond Barnes's only heir was big news. Only her family pedigree wasn't good enough for my grandfather. He went to her and offered her a lot of money to break it off."

"Did she?"

He stuck the revolver in the holster on his hip.

"Yes. A week before the wedding, she and her family moved to another city and into a very fancy home."

"That's terrible. How could she do that?"

"I imagine my grandfather made it plain that he controlled the money and if she had any hopes of getting her family out of the ghetto, his was a one time offer."

Reaching out, Jennifer laid a hand on his arm. Her touch comforted him. "That was a terrible thing for them to do, but you need to forgive them."

"You're saying I should just forget that they made my life miserable? That's not possible."

"You're right. Forgetting such a betrayal isn't possible, but *forgiving* such a betrayal is. Once you find it in your heart to forgive Miranda and your grandfather, you take away the power their act has to hurt you."

Shaking his head, he managed a wry smile. "No. It seems my grandfather isn't the only one with too much pride."

A pensive look clouded her eyes. She took a few steps away to brace her hands on the fence. He watched her with concern. Something was troubling her.

"Ready to tell me about your *au naturel* shopping trip?"

She smiled at him over her shoulder. "I was twelve months old. I apparently escaped from my mother's clutches by crawling under the produce table where I shed my diaper and my top and took off like the gleeful toddler I was. My father chased me down and caught me before I had time to shock the checkout line. He really enjoyed telling that story."

Avery chuckled. "I can imagine he would."

"You wouldn't think twice about embarrassing your own daughter with that story in front of her junior high prom date, would you?" she demanded.

It was easy to imagine a small blond toddler with Jennifer's bright blue eyes and dimpled cheeks getting into trouble right and left. For the first time he considered what stories he might share with children of his own.

"I wish I could have met your father."

She sighed wistfully. "I wish you could have, too. You would have enjoyed his sense of humor. I know death isn't the end, but there are so many things I would have liked to tell him."

Turning away from the fence, she faced Avery. "That's why I'm going to tell you something now that I said I wouldn't."

She shifted nervously from one foot to the other.

"I'm listening," Avery said, worried by her intensity.

"Your grandfather is ill. He's already had one heart attack and a triple bypass surgery."

"How do you know that?" Avery demanded. Was this some kind of trick his grandfather had gotten Jennifer to pull on him?

Quickly, she said, "The first day I met him, after you had left him in the stable, I found him slumped over and in need of a nitroglycerin tablet. He was having chest pain. I thought he was having a heart attack. I wanted to get you or call 9-1-1, but he wouldn't let me."

"He was faking it." His grandfather was made of granite. He'd never been sick a day in his life.

Shaking her head, she said, "You can't fake those kinds of symptoms. He was flushed and sweating. If his pills hadn't helped right away I would have called for an ambulance. He told me he wants to reconcile with you—but I don't think he knows how to start."

Avery took a few steps away. To clear his head. To wrap his mind around what she was saying. "I don't believe it."

"I'm sorry." The sympathy in her voice told him she believed it was true.

He waited, wanting to feel gladness or at least satisfaction that Edmond was facing something he couldn't buy off or bribe his way out of—only those weren't the emotions that came. Instead, sorrow crept in and then pity. For all his money, Edmond was alone now, without family or true friends to stand beside him.

"I used to want to be like him. I *am* like him," Avery admitted slowly.

Coming to his side, Jennifer took his hand and held it between hers. Her warmth drove the chill from his mind. "You don't have to repeat his mistakes. You can be your own man."

Looking down into her eyes, Avery had a glimpse of what the future could be like if she were always beside him. She was an anchor to everyone around her. But why would she have him? He didn't share her faith or her values. She deserved so much more from the man who loved her.

And he did love her.

He loved her bright eyes and the way she threw herself into solving the problems life handed her—even if they weren't her problems. He reached up and brushed a lock of hair back from her face. "Is that another one of Jennifer's top ten tips to positive living?"

Her smile was as soft as the evening breeze. "It's number five."

"Someday maybe you can give me the whole list."

"What would you do with it? Tattoo it on your forehead?"

He flicked her nose with the tip of his finger. "I'd tattoo it on yours. That way I wouldn't have to look in the mirror each time I needed a reminder."

"What makes you think I'll be around when you need a reminder?"

"Good point."

Did that mean she wasn't interested in seeing him once their training sessions were done? He wanted to ask, but he wasn't sure he wanted to hear her answer. Not yet, anyway.

"What are you going to do about your grandfather?"

"Nothing."

Jennifer bit her lip, appalled that her breach of confidence didn't make any difference to Avery. She dropped his hand. "How can you say that?"

"It was easy. I opened my mouth and the words came out." He drew the reloaded gun and held it out to her.

Taking it, she started to turn away, but he reached out and gripped her arm. "I know you want to help, but my family isn't like yours. There isn't any respect or love for one another lurking under the surface. I'm sorry he's sick, but it doesn't change a lifetime of making me feel like I'm his biggest disappointment since learning Santa doesn't exist."

"I'm sorry you were made to feel that way. I just thought you should know he was ill." Blinking back tears of disillusionment, she looked down. All this time she thought Avery's indifference toward people was an act. Perhaps it wasn't. She wanted him to be so much more.

"You can't fix everyone, Jenny."

"I know." She pulled free of his hand and walked toward the next target. Raising the gun, she blasted the balloon to pieces.

"Jenny?"

"What?" She glanced toward him. His smile was incredibly sad. "Don't stop trying."

Heartened, she smiled back. "I don't intend to."

Later that evening, after he had finished instructing Jennifer in the finer points of shooting from horseback and returned Dakota to the stables, Avery found himself once again parked in front of the bed and breakfast in Dutton. Getting out of his car, he stood staring at the building and wondering what he was going to say to his grandfather.

The front door opened and the man he was thinking about came out. Tonight Edmond had a cane in his hand and he leaned on it heavily as he started down the sidewalk. When he caught sight of Avery, he paused.

Avery stayed where he was and after a few seconds Edmond walked toward him. "It's such a nice night, I thought I would take a little stroll before I went to bed. Would you care to join me?"

Not knowing what else to do, Avery agreed. "I guess."

The two men fell into step together, Avery shortening his stride to match the older man's. An awkward silence stretched between them.

The small town was quiet, with only an occasional car going past. The sounds of cicadas and crickets filled the air as they walked beneath the maples and oaks lining the street. Lights shone from the windows of the two-story Victorian homes on both sides of the avenue and occasional voices reached them. A dog in the neighbor's yard began barking, setting off a canine chorus chain reaction down the block.

"This place seems like something out of Currier and Ives," Edmond said at last. "It's obvious the people here take a lot of pride in their town."

"It's okay for Hicksville."

"You young people don't have an appreciation for things of the past century. You're always in a hurry. You want instant everything. Instant oatmeal, instant messaging, instant gratification. Good things take time."

He hadn't come to discuss the vices or the virtues of modern times. Avery said, "Jennifer told me you've been sick."

"I thought as much when I saw you tonight. I must admit I'm surprised that she didn't share that information sooner. According to her mother, she has a very tender heart."

"I hope you aren't planning to use them to get to me."

Edmond stopped and turned to face Avery. "Why are you here?"

"I've been asking myself that same question."

"If you've come to gloat, I don't blame you. I treated you badly." Edmond clenched his fingers and raised his fist. "I thought hardness would make you hard and that would somehow protect you in this cutthroat world."

"From cutthroats like you?"

Edmond's hand fell to his side. "Yes."

"What do you want from me?" Avery asked calmly, keeping his anger and pity out of his voice.

A lopsided smile lifted the corner of Edmond's mouth. "All I want is for you to accompany me on the rest of my stroll this evening. Is that too much to ask?"

He didn't wait for Avery to reply, but began walking.

Avery almost turned around and left. When he realized his hands were clenched into fists at his sides, he relaxed them. If he left now, he'd lose any chance of getting to the bottom of Edmond's plans.

Catching up with his grandfather, he walked beside him in silence until they reached the end of the block. Edmond turned left and continued on.

"My doctor has instructed me to walk for forty minutes twice a day. It's amazing how much you see when you take the time to just walk."

"How sick are you?" Avery asked.

Edmond glanced at him. "According to my cardiologist I may have a few more years. Five if I take care of myself."

"I'm sorry," Avery said quietly.

"Don't be. I'm already eighty years old. Five more would be quite a gift."

"Who is running the firm while you're here?"

"I'd rather not talk about work, if you don't mind."

"That's a switch." Avery almost laughed out loud.

"Yes. My work was my addiction. It cost me my family, my friends, more than you know."

The regret in his grandfather's tone sounded genuine, but Avery wasn't ready to believe it. "You reaped plenty of rewards from your labor."

Edmond stopped and stared at the ground. Quietly, he said, "Yes, I gathered a large amount of wealth. The root of all evil. I thank God I've been given a chance to change and to know Him."

Giving his head a slight shake, he started forward again. "Mrs. Grant told me that you've been helping her daughter learn swordsmanship. Are you really?"

Changing the subject wasn't what Avery wanted, but he went along with it. "Yes. Jennifer is taking part in the town's re-enactment of some woman's charge into the face of certain death."

"The renowned Henrietta Dutton?"

"You've heard of her?"

Edmond chuckled. "Not until I came here. The owners of the bed and breakfast have quite an extensive knowledge of the woman. Apparently Mrs. Marcus is a direct descendent."

"Did you tell her one of our ancestors participated in the Boston Tea Party?"

"I thought about it, but decided my breakfast toast might end up burnt if I one-upped her genealogy. Mrs. Marcus is quite touchy on the subject. On the other hand, Miss Grant seems like a very nice young woman. From something she said I gather you have known each other for a while."

"Jennifer is great. She's—genuine."

"Do I detect an interest on your part?"

"I'd rather leave her out of this conversation."

"Of course. I didn't mean to pry."

They continued walking in silence until they turned the corner toward the inn.

Edmond cleared his throat. "I see we're almost back where we started from."

"I guess we are." Nothing had been solved between them. Avery still didn't know what to make of Edmond's presence. Was it possible his grandfather had come to make peace between them? Mulling over the possibility, Avery didn't discard the notion as he would have a week ago. Something about Edmond was different.

At the sidewalk leading to the front of the bed and breakfast, Edmond stopped and faced Avery. "Thank you for your company tonight."

"You haven't told me why you're hanging around this one-horse town."

"I'm hoping to discover something."

"About me?"

"About myself. Goodnight, Avery. Perhaps I'll see you at the festival."

Watching his grandfather walk away and enter the house, Avery struggled with a multitude of conflicting emotions. He had spent years detesting the man and trying his best to make his grandfather detest him in return. Yet deep underneath his anger and resentment had always been a childish longing to be loved and respected by the old man.

Avery wasn't sure he wanted to give up his anger. It gave him purpose. But that purpose had led him to behave in ways he wasn't proud of, in ways Jennifer could never approve of.

If he changed—if he wanted to become the kind of man she could respect and care for—he would have to start here. He would have to find it in his heart to forgive. And to ask forgiveness in return.

He knew with sudden clarity that it would be the hardest task he had ever faced.

Chapter Fifteen

Jennifer was reading her homework while mixing the ingredients for a casserole the next day when she heard Avery drive in. She bit her lip as she struggled to keep her battered emotions under control. She had spent a long night in soul searching and personal inventory and she still didn't know how she was going to handle her growing affection for him.

The smart thing would be to stop seeing him all together, but she had promised to coach him until the cavalry competition was over. It was still a week away. Seven days of looking into Avery's dark eyes, of seeing the roguish smile that sent her heart skipping, of wanting to be held in his arms.

"Help me, Lord," she whispered. "I know what is right. I know he's not the kind of man

I need in my life, but I can't change how I feel. Show me what You want me to do."

"Are you talking to yourself, Jennifer?" Mary inquired as she crossed the living room on her crutches.

Jennifer felt a blush heat her face. "Actually, I was talking to God."

"He's the best listener in the universe, of course, but I'm available, too. Is there anything I can do to help?"

"No, I'm okay. Thanks." The last thing her mother needed was to start worrying about Jennifer's love life.

Jennifer slipped the green-and-white glass pan into the oven, set the timer, then checked out the kitchen window. She saw Toby and Ryan helping Avery unload Dakota. The three of them seemed caught up in earnest conversation. Lollypop was already saddled and waiting for her inside the corral. There was no reason to hurry outside, except that she wanted to be with him.

Jennifer felt a hand on her shoulder and she turned to her mother. Mary's eyes were brimming with understanding and love.

"I'm not unfamiliar with troubles of the heart, dear," Mary said quietly. "Are you sure you don't want to talk about it?"

Sighing, Jennifer battled the sting of tears. "I like him so much and I know how wrong that is."

"Why is it wrong to care about someone?"

"Because *he's* all wrong. He doesn't share our faith, he doesn't have principles or honor. He thinks money is the answer to everything. He isn't a bit like Daddy."

"You're being rather harsh, aren't you?"

"The truth is harsh in his case."

"Jennifer, if there wasn't something—special—about that young man, we wouldn't be having this conversation. What is it that you see in him?"

"I don't know what I see in him, except…"

"Except what?"

"Sometimes, I think I see how much pain he is in."

"So you feel sympathy?"

Shaking her head vigorously, Jennifer was quick to deny that accusation. "No, quite the opposite. I want to shake him and tell him to wake up and take a look around. There is so much good in the world and he's making himself unhappy by his choices."

"And you are making yourself unhappy… because?"

"I didn't choose to be unhappy. I didn't

choose to fall for a guy that would let me down—twice—or as many times as I let him."

"I'm going to tell you something you already know. A woman who clings to a man in hopes of changing him is destined for a life of heartache."

"I do know that."

"Good. Now I'm going to tell you something you don't know. Before I met your father, he had been to church less than a dozen times in his life. He was my father's nightmare. Good looking, charming and as wild as the hills."

"Dad?" Jennifer wasn't sure she believed what she was hearing. Her father had been a rock of faith and love.

"Yes. He was a sorry case."

"So what changed him?"

"Wanting my love more than anything and knowing that he had it in himself to attain it."

"I don't understand."

"I made it plain to your father that I cared about him, but that I deserved the kind of husband God wanted me to have. I wouldn't settle for anything less. Your father knew that to marry me he was going to have to become that man."

"And that brought him to God?"

"Not right away, but it got his attention."

"Avery thinks religion is a joke."

"Not everyone finds God in a flash of revelation as it happened to the Apostle Paul. People who quietly seek faith through study and through prayer, those people find Him, too. Your father started going to church because I said he should. In time, and by God's grace, he found salvation."

"I hardly think Avery will start attending church because I ask him. In fact, I'm pretty sure he'll say no thanks."

"Then let him say it and show him that what you value can't be cast aside. Follow your own heart. If he isn't the man you think he can be, then God will show you that. Have faith in yourself and in him."

"Thanks, Mom. Are you going to come out and watch me practice?" Her mother had given her a lot to consider.

Mary shook her head. Some of the light left her eyes. "No. I don't think so."

"I've got skills. Even Avery says I'm doing better than he expected."

"I'm sure you are, but I think I'm going to rest for a while."

Jennifer remembered with a sinking heart that her mother had wanted to be the one to make the historic ride. "Of course. Is your leg hurting?"

"No more than usual. I'm just a little tired.

They worked me over pretty good in therapy today."

"I'm so glad Mr. Marcus is able to drive you to your appointment. I've been worrying how I was going to get you there and get back to class on time."

"Yes, it was sweet of Pastor McGregor to ask for volunteers to help us, but Mr. Marcus couldn't make it this morning."

Jennifer cocked her head to the side. "Then who took you?"

"Mr. Barnes was kind enough to take me. Actually, it was his driver who took us. I felt quite special being dropped off by a chauffeur at the clinic."

"I imagine."

"Avery's grandfather is quite taken with you."

"With me?" Jennifer wasn't sure if she was more surprised by the comment or by the fact that her mother had spent the morning in Mr. Barnes's company.

"Yes. He seems to feel that you're a good influence on Avery."

Jennifer hesitated, not sure how much Avery would appreciate her sharing his family troubles. Still, it seemed best to let her mother know how things stood. "Avery and his grandfather are estranged."

"Yes, it's very sad, but Mr. Barnes is hopeful that they can heal the breach. Especially since Avery has taken the next step."

"The next step?"

"Yes, he went to visit his grandfather last night. I think family feuds are the saddest kind, don't you? If someone doesn't have the love and support of those who should be the closest to them, it must leave them feeling rudderless."

"I can't believe Mr. Barnes discussed his family problems with you. I mean, you're practically strangers."

"He doesn't seem like a stranger, he seems like someone I've known a long time. Anyway, I had the feeling he wanted me to understand that Avery wasn't entirely to blame for his... unwise lifestyle choices."

Avery had made poor choices, but Jennifer couldn't help being proud of the choice he had made yesterday. It proved he was willing to change if he had gone to see his grandfather. The hope she had been trying so hard to weed out of her heart blossomed like an early spring crocus.

"Mother, do you like Avery?"

"Dear, the real question is do you like him?"

"A lot. I like him very much."

"And does he like you?"

Jennifer tipped her head to the side as she considered her mother's question. "I believe he does."

"Then don't be afraid. Nurture that affection and trust God to see where it leads."

Standing inside the corral where he had already set up the balloons and burlap bags, Avery was engaged in trying to cheer up Ryan when Jennifer came around the corner of the barn. The sad youngster who knew Isabella was going back to her owner in the morning was forgotten as Avery took in the wide smile on Jennifer's face and the sparkle in her eyes.

For once she looked happy to see him. Not just happy, she looked positively delighted.

She was wearing another prairie skirt. This one was gray with pink bows around the hem. Without breaking stride, she came right up to him, rose on tiptoe and planted a kiss on his cheek.

Not quite sure what to make of her behavior, he asked cautiously, "What was that for?"

"Just because."

"Yuck!" Ryan scrunched up his nose. "Don't do that mushy stuff."

"Pay no attention to the kid," Avery countered quickly. "Do all the mushy stuff you want."

She giggled. "I think we'd better get to work." Smiling at him, she said, "Now fall down dead."

"I'm weak in the knees, but not that weak," he assured her.

Batting his chest, she said, "You're Colonel Dutton. Fall down dead so I can pick up your sword and gun and ride into history. Come on, I've only got three days left to get this right."

Grinning, he stepped back and pressed both hands to his chest. "I'm hit."

He staggered a few feet to the left and spun around once. "They've killed me, Henrietta."

He staggered a few steps to the right. "Don't let my dream die with me."

Ryan began laughing uncontrollably.

Dropping to his knees, Avery drew his sword and held it aloft. "Fight on," he croaked and fell face down in the dirt.

Jennifer chuckled as she pulled his sidearm out of his holster, then tried to pull his saber from his hand. He held on tight.

"Let go," she muttered, pulling harder.

"You have to pry it from my cold dead hand," he whispered.

She rapped his knuckles with something hard.

"Ouch." He lifted his head to see her holding the butt of the gun like a hammer over his fingers. He let loose.

Pistol in her right hand, saber in her left, she headed for Lollypop. The little black mare was watching the whole performance with wide-eyed interest.

Avery propped his chin on his hands. "Lines!"

Jennifer stopped. "Something, something, can't kill a dream."

Grabbing the horse's reins, she swung into the saddle and charged down the fence line. She missed the first target she fired at, but managed to hit the second one.

Avery jumped to his feet to watch. Dropping the pistol, Jennifer switched the saber to her right hand, narrowly missing Lollypop's ears in the maneuver. The rest of her charge proved she had been practicing as she hit all but one burlap bag.

The course brought her around the corral and back to Avery, where she drew Lollypop to a stop and pointed the saber at him.

"Surrender or die."

Looking into her incredibly blue eyes, he knew she had captured his heart. He held up his hands. "I surrender. I'm yours if you'll have me."

Lowering the tip of her sword, she nudged her horse close to him. He saw uncertainty settle over her delicate features. "Do you mean that?"

Sensing her seriousness, he said, "I do, Jennifer. I never felt this way about anyone. Will you give me another chance?"

She tipped her head to the side. "Yes, Corporal Barnes, I believe I will."

He breathed a sigh of relief. He had no idea what had made her change her mind today, but he was going to take advantage of it. "You won't be sorry, sweetheart. I promise you that."

She stepped down from the horse and smiled shyly. "I'm going to hold you to that. You and I are going to have some long talks. There are things you need to know and understand before we go any further with this relationship. Things I won't compromise on."

"Such as?"

"My faith and what that means for the two of us."

"All right. I promise I'll listen with an open mind."

"That's all I can ask."

"You are one special girl." Capturing both her hands, Avery smiled down at her, feeling happier than he could ever remember.

Chapter Sixteen

The morning of the Founders' Day Festival dawned bright and clear. Jennifer peeked out her bedroom window at a few minutes after six in the morning and groaned. Apparently a torrential flood or early blizzard wasn't going to get her off the hook. She would have to make her charge up Dutton Heights.

Turning off her alarm a minute before it was set to start blaring music, she wondered if Henrietta Dutton was spinning in her grave.

The dress rehearsal the day before had been a disaster. Not only had Jennifer missed all but one of her targets, but Lollypop had repeatedly refused the final jump at the top of the hill leaving the actor playing the brigand leader unable to surrender to anyone.

Edna Marcus had broken down in tears and

declared she wouldn't be a party to making a mockery of her great, great, great aunt's bravery.

When Jennifer walked into the kitchen, she saw the rest of her family already gathered around the table. The silence was deafening.

Plopping down in her chair, Jennifer began buttering a slice of toast. "You don't have to stop talking about me just because I'm here. I can take it."

Ryan, a smear of strawberry jam on his cheek, leaned toward her. "Lizzie said you messed up big time."

"Tattle tale," Lizzie growled, kicking him under the table.

"Well, she's right," Jennifer agreed. "I'm sorry, Mom. I'll try to do better today."

"You'll do fine," Mary reassured her, but Jennifer could tell she was worried. Her mother had been watching from the sidelines and Jennifer felt the weight of her disappointment.

"I did great the day before when Avery and I went over the course."

She had been so proud of her skills that she had actually been looking forward to demonstrating them in front of the crowds that would be there today. Now it looked as if her accuracy had been a fluke.

At least Avery hadn't been there to witness

her paltry effort yesterday. His duties at the fort had kept him away from the dress rehearsal, but he had promised to be at the festival today. She would need a hug from him before and after she made a fool of herself.

Toby patted her shoulder. "You'll do fine, sis. Shake it off."

Ryan jumped to his feet and flapped his hands wildly. "Yeah, shake it off like this."

"Finish your breakfast, Ryan." His mother's stern tone sent him meekly back to his chair. The rest of the meal passed in silence. Jennifer choked down her toast, but it didn't settle her butterflies.

It was nearly nine o'clock when they arrived at the grassy area cordoned off for the numerous horse trailers and campers belonging to the re-enactors. Many of them had been camped at the site since the middle of the week.

She moved quickly to help her mother out of the truck. Mary, dressed in her favorite blue plaid gown, scowled at the crutches Lizzie handed her.

"I wish I didn't need them. They spoil the look of this dress."

Jennifer said, "I don't care. If you don't use them, then I am taking you home."

"She will, too," Lizzie added, slipping out

after her mother. Having opted for a modern look, she was wearing green twill pants with a matching white-and-green striped shirt beneath a tan jacket.

"Can we go to the concessions stand?" Toby asked as he climbed out from the rear seat.

"Yeah. I'm hungry, too," Ryan added, trying unsuccessfully to look like a starving waif.

"You can't be hungry already. You only finished breakfast an hour ago," Jennifer pointed out.

"We are," Ryan insisted.

Mary glanced toward one of the white tents set up nearby. "All right, but be back here in ten minutes. We don't want to miss the performance."

"Thanks, Mom," the boys echoed each other, then raced away.

"Lizzie, go keep an eye on them," Mary said.

"Do I have to?"

"Yes." Her mother's tone didn't allow for argument. Lizzie rolled her eyes, but did as she was told.

"I'd like to miss the performance," Jennifer muttered.

Mary shook her head sadly. "And waste all the time you've put into learning how to shoot and wield a sword? When are you ever going to use those skills again if not today?"

"Never. Next year it will be you making this ride." Walking to the rear of the horse trailer, Jennifer opened the door and backed out Lollypop. The mare was already saddled and ready to make her famous run.

Glancing toward the nearby hilltop, Mary sighed. "I hope it's part of God's plan for me, but some things are more important. If I can't ride again, then I can't."

Patting Lollypop's neck, Jennifer glanced at her mother's sad face. Sudden worry struck her. "Mom, you told me the doctor said your knee is getting better."

Mary straightened and managed a smile that didn't quite reach her eyes. "Yes, but I do wish I could be out there today. Since I can't, I'm really glad that it's you."

"You've never told me why this thing is so important to you. If I'm going to go out and make a fool of myself, I think I should know why."

Mary looked down. "My zeal must seem silly to you."

Jennifer studied her mother's face. "A little, but I'd like to know why it means so much to you."

Looking up, Mary met her daughter's gaze. "When your father died, I thought the world ended. You remember how I was. I knew I should be taking care of you children, but I couldn't find the strength. I was in a deep, dark well and I didn't have the courage to climb out. I'm so ashamed of how weak I was, how weak my faith was then."

"Mom, you weren't weak. You were grieving. There is a difference."

"Perhaps, but Henrietta Dutton, a woman who was the same age I was, who had children, who saw her husband shot down in front of her eyes, didn't give in to grief. Unlike me, she did something incredibly brave. She acted the way I wish I had been able to act when your father died."

Tears glistened in Mary's eyes. "I wish I had been as brave for you."

Throwing her arms around her mother, Jennifer hugged her fiercely. "You are every bit as brave as Henrietta was. It just took you a little longer to find that strength, but I see it every day, and I am so proud of you."

Mary returned the hug, then, leaning back on her crutches, she reached up to pat Jennifer's face. "Thank you, sweetie. Now go out there and show the world what kind of strength lurked in the heart of a woman history has overlooked. There were a lot more women like her and their stories deserve to be told."

Jennifer wiped at the tears on her cheeks. "You make me wish I had practiced harder."

"You'll do fine," a deep, familiar masculine voice stated firmly. "You had a good teacher."

Jennifer looked up to see Avery watching her. Mounted on Dakota and dressed in his cavalry uniform, Avery managed to look more handsome than ever. The reassuring smile on his face gave her lagging courage a much needed boost. "Let's hope I was a good pupil."

All around them, men and women in period costumes, some on horseback or in horse-drawn wagons, were taking their places on the green. Several roped off areas held back the growing crowds who had come to watch. The mayor stepped up to the microphone on a raised platform.

Mary made shooing motions with one hand. "You two should get to your places."

Avery touched his hat in a brief salute. "Yes, ma'am. Will you be all right here alone?"

"Actually, your grandfather will be keeping the children and me company. I see him heading this way." She raised her hand to wave.

Glancing at Avery, Jennifer saw he looked as surprised as she was.

Turning in the saddle, Avery regarded his grandfather's approach with a stoic face. Jennifer couldn't read his expression. She didn't know what he was thinking, but at least there was no sign of the anger that had marked their previous meetings when she was present.

Edmond, looking dapper in a dark blue blazer with a red tie, stopped beside the group. He nodded toward his grandson. "Avery, I'm looking forward to seeing your unit in action. I've heard great things about it."

"Thank you, sir. We'll try not to disappoint."

Relieved that the two were at least speaking to each other, Jennifer breathed a prayer of thanks. "I appreciate your staying with my mother, sir."

"It's my pleasure. I'm sure the pageant will be that much more enjoyable for me due to her keen knowledge of the events themselves."

Mary actually blushed. "Edmond was able to reserve seats for us in the viewing stand with the mayor and the rest of the town council. We'd best be going, too."

Smiling at Mr. Barnes with gratitude, Jennifer glanced up at Avery. He leaned toward her and said softly, "Go knock 'em dead, Jenny."

"I will."

She mounted her horse and galloped across the short distance to a buggy waiting several dozen yards away. A group of men on horseback dressed as farmers from the 1850s were already gathered beside it. Jennifer tied Lollypop to the rear of the wagon and allowed Gerard Hoover, the grocer turned Colonel for the day, to assist her up to the black leather seat.

Avery watched Jennifer ride away with a heady mixture of pride and love surging through him. He wanted her to succeed as much as he had wanted anything in a long time.

Please, God, if You bother listening to some- one like me, I'd like to ask a favor. Let her do well today.

Feeling a bit self-conscious about his attempt at prayer, he turned Dakota and rode back to where his unit was forming up. Maneuvering into position beside his fellow soldiers, he accepted the unit's banner from Lee. Beside him, Sergeant Stone held the U.S. flag.

The mayor of Dutton tapped the microphone and began to speak. "Welcome, ladies and gen- tlemen, to our Founders' Day Festival and the first recreation of the brave and selfless acts of a husband and wife who helped found our fair city.

"In the days before the great Civil War, our state, referred to by many as Bloody Kansas, had become a war zone. Colonel Arthur Dutton was a firm believer that slavery was a sin. He was instrumental in aiding many escaped slaves and he was determined to see that Kansas entered the Union as a free state. He and four other brave men died here when Bushwhackers attacked this cabin where an escaped slave and his family were in hiding."

Avery found himself listening with interest to the mayor's tale. He realized for the first time that the land he stood on had been stained with the blood of men who valued freedom more than life. Freedom not for themselves, but for others. The knowledge was humbling. He glanced at the men beside him and saw the same look of reverence on their faces.

"Even as Colonel Dutton fell," the mayor continued, "his wife took up his sword and rallied his remaining men by charging into the teeth of the enemy. We are here to bear witness to that bravery."

The mayor paused for breath and Sergeant Stone said quietly, "Prepare to move out."

Avery tightened his grip on the staff of the company's banner. He was here as a representative of all the men and women who served their country in the army. He was here to honor them.

"To begin our celebration," the mayor said with a flourish, "the Dutton High School band will perform the national anthem as Fort Riley's own Commanding General's Mounted Color Guard brings in our flag."

The band began to play. As the stirring notes reached out across the hillside, Avery's unit moved forward at a solemn walk. In two rows of four abreast, they made a circuit before the crowds. The restless wind tugged at the Stars and Stripes, causing the flag to ripple and flutter. Even the matching bay horses, heads held low, seemed to sense the somber mood.

By the end of the song, the unit had made a complete circle and stopped in front of the mayor's platform. The second row of riders moved up, forming a single row.

"Present Arms," Sergeant Stone barked. The rasp of sabers leaving their scabbards filled the air and sunlight glinted off the blades as the men raised their swords to touch the brims of their hats, then sliced them down to rest beside their boots.

On a second command, Avery nudged Dakota into motion and the line split into columns of twos. Catching the eye of the rider across from him, Avery kicked Dakota into a gallop. The columns separated and turned outward forming a circle, then raced back toward each other, passing in between one another at a run. The crowd erupted into applause.

* * *

Jennifer watched the display of military horsemanship with the same awe that moved the crowd of festival goers to thunderous applause. Tears of pride pricked the backs of her eyes. But all too quickly the unit's ride was done and she had to turn her attention from Avery to her upcoming part. Gerard slapped the team into motion and the buggy jerked forward.

At the cabin, Jennifer allowed her pretend husband to assist her in alighting, then made her way to knock on the cabin door. Inside, she waited breathlessly for her cue. It didn't take long. Suddenly the quiet hillside erupted with the sounds of gunfire.

With her heart in her throat and a prayer on her lips that God wouldn't let her make a complete fool out of herself, Jennifer gathered her skirts and ran out of the log cabin to her fallen husband's side.

She dropped to her knees and pulled Mr. Hoover's bald head into her lap. The sounds of gunfire echoed all around her and puffs of blue smoke drifted through the air. She could see Avery standing in the crowd at the roped off area a few yards away.

"Good luck," Gerard whispered from the

side of his mouth, his eyes tightly closed in pretend death.

"Thanks," she whispered back as she gently laid his head on the ground. Snatching the saber from his hand, she rose to her feet, held it overhead and froze.

Oh, what is my line? Think.

"Bullets can't…" he prompted softly.

"Bullets can't stop his dream," she yelled, grateful to the make-believe corpse at her feet.

"Take the gun," he growled softly.

She had almost forgotten that part. Stooping, she snatched up the pistol and stuffed it in the waistband of her skirt. Turning, she raced toward Lollypop, still tied to the wagon. Jerking the reins free, she stuck her foot in the stirrup and everything else became automatic.

Crouching low over the mare's neck, Jennifer pulled out her gun and fired off a round at the first bandit's silhouette. To her immense relief, it fell backward as planned. She heard the rallying cry of the men behind her, but didn't allow it to break her concentration. The next marauder fell, too. Dropping the pistol, she raised the saber and urged Lollypop up the hillside. All of the manikins dressed as Bushwhackers fell over when her blade struck them. At the very top of the hill, Lollypop leaped lightly over a small split rail fence and Jennifer brandished her sword toward the last Bushwhacker hiding there.

"Surrender or die!" she shouted.

He threw down his weapon and raised his hands. Seconds later, the rest of Colonel Dutton's men swarmed over the fence and subdued him.

Twisting around in the saddle, Jennifer searched for Avery in the crowd below. She wanted to share her triumph with him more than with anyone. He had made this possible. She scanned the faces but didn't see him. What she did see was a girl in a green striped top and green pants break out of the crowd and begin running up the hill. She recognized Lizzie and her heart stood still at the look of panic on her sister's face.

Wheeling Lollypop, Jennifer kicked the mare into motion and raced down the hill. She reached her sister in a matter of seconds. Slipping from the saddle, she grasped Lizzie by the shoulders. "Liz, what's wrong?"

"It's Mom. She's fainted."

"Fainted? Did someone call 9-1-1? Where is she?"

"On the reviewing stand. There's a doctor with her. Mr. Barnes sent me to get you."

Jennifer hiked up her skirts and began running toward a cluster of people grouped at one end of the platform. She was relieved to see Avery was one of them. Quickly climbing the steps, she rushed to where Mary Grant was still lying on the wooden floor.

Jennifer recognized the man helping her mother as the young doctor from the hospital emergency room. Dropping to her knees beside her mother, she tried to control the fear in her voice. "Mom, are you all right?"

"I'm fine," Mary insisted as she attempted to sit upright. "I simply stood too quickly."

The doctor scowled at his patient. "You need to get out of that corset. It's restricting your breathing. They went out of style for a reason."

Jennifer, struggling to catch her own breath, agreed with his assertion. "He's right."

"Yes, I know." Mary reached out and cupped Jennifer's cheek. "You were magnificent, dear. I'm so proud of you."

"I'm glad you were conscious to see it. Can you get up?"

Avery and the doctor lifted her into a nearby chair. Mary winced and grabbed her leg.

"Did you hurt your knee, Mrs. Grant?" the doctor asked.

"I may have twisted it a little," she admitted with a pain-filled grimace.

"You know it's not going to get better until you have surgery," he said, shaking his head.

Mary glanced at Jennifer, then bit her lip and looked away.

Jennifer's gaze moved from her mother's face to the doctor. "But I thought you said she didn't need surgery."

He didn't say anything, but Jennifer could see that he wanted to. She stared at her mother. "Mom, why would you tell us you were getting better if you weren't?"

"I'm doing fine."

Jennifer sat back on her heels and pressed a hand to her forehead. "You think we can't afford it. You're not having surgery so I can stay in school."

"Your future is more important than my living with a little limp."

Jennifer rose to her feet and faced the doctor. "Exactly what is her prognosis?"

"I'm sorry. I can't discuss it without the patient's permission."

Rounding on her mother, Jennifer propped her hands on her hips and glared at her. "Then you tell me what he said."

Edmond stepped up and laid a hand on Mary's shoulder. "I'm not bound by any vows of confidentiality. He told her that unless she has surgery soon, it was unlikely that she'll ever ride again."

"Edmond, I wish you hadn't. I was upset when I shared that with you." Mary looked ready to cry.

"I'm sorry, my dear, but your daughter deserves to know."

Jennifer sank onto the chair next to her mother and took her hand. "Mom, you love riding as much as I do. I couldn't let you give that up just to stay in school another semester."

"No, you can't quit. I know how it is. Once you leave school you'll never go back. That's what happened to me and I've always regretted it. No. I won't discuss it further. Let's go home. I don't want your wonderful performance today marred by my silliness. Avery, hand me my crutches, please."

He did, but when she tried to rise, her legs buckled and she sat back with a groan. The doctor knelt in front of her and carefully lifted her full skirt to expose her injured knee. He palpated it gently, but his touch brought tears to her eyes.

"The patella is definitely out of place now," the doctor said. "I'm sorry, Mrs. Grant, but I think the decision has been made for you. You're going to need surgery as soon as possible."

"And don't even think about refusing!" Jennifer added. Mary nodded meekly.

Rising to her feet, Jennifer looked into Avery's sympathetic eyes and almost cried herself.

She drew a deep breath. "Avery, do you think you could get some of the men to help carry my mother to my truck if I pull up next to the steps?"

"Sure, and don't worry about Lollypop, or the boys. I'll see that everyone gets home."

"Thank you." Jennifer had actually forgotten about the little mare who was standing quietly exactly where Jennifer had dropped the reins. Her brothers were standing at the edge of the platform with wide, worried eyes.

Avery pulled her close in a quick hug. "It's going to be all right."

"I know."

It would be all right if this was God's plan for them. Next year she would pick up her studies where she left off and her mother would be fully recovered and able to make her ride up Dutton Heights.

Next year. If it was God's plan for them.

Chapter Seventeen

Avery was at the fort's large corral late Monday afternoon when he saw Jennifer's truck pull up beside the fence. He wanted to race over and take her in his arms, but he managed to control the impulse with difficulty. Walking sedately to where she stood was hard, but once she was within reach, he couldn't help himself. She looked so tired and lonely. He wrapped his arms around her and she melted into his embrace.

He kissed the top of her head. "How's it going?"

"Okay, I guess. Do you have a few minutes?"

Looking over his shoulder, he saw Sergeant Stone nod once. Avery nodded his thanks in return, then said, "Sure. What do you need?"

"I just wanted to see you." Her simple statement touched something deep inside him and made his love for her grow.

Drawing back, he cupped her face in his hands. "Here I am."

She gave him a tired smile. "I feel better already."

He wanted to kiss her but he was aware of the men in his unit watching them. "How's your mother?"

"Good. The surgery went well yesterday."

"I'm sorry I couldn't be there. We were in Tulsa for a rodeo. I couldn't get leave on such short notice."

He took her hand and they began to walk toward the shady banks of a creek just beyond the fences.

She sent him a sidelong glance. "You're a soldier. I understand that you have duties you can't just drop. Besides, we weren't alone. Your grandfather has been in to visit every day."

"Really?" He wasn't sure what to make of that information.

"Have you had another chance to talk to him?"

"Not since the festival, but I'd rather hear about you than about him. Did you notify the school that you're dropping your classes?"

"Not yet. I don't know why I'm dragging my feet."

"Jennifer, I can help with the money."

Stopping, she quickly turned to face him and placed a hand on his lips. "I know you can, but I couldn't accept it. You know that."

Grasping her wrist gently, he moved her hand from his mouth and placed it over his heart. "Did anyone ever tell you that you're as stubborn as a little donkey?"

"No, but someone once mentioned I had big ears and a long nose…how did that go?"

"A nose you poked into everyone else's business. I guess I should apologize for that remark."

"That's a fine idea."

"If you apologize for telling that cute second-year vet student that I was ungodly."

Holding up one finger, she wagged it in front of his face. "I never told her that, and she wasn't that cute."

"Jennifer, tell the truth."

Turning away, she started walking again, pulling him along by the hand she still held. "Okay, she was very cute."

"And?"

"I told her you thought religion was a joke and to steer clear of you. She told the other girls."

"Now that I'm going to church, would you tell her I'm available and acceptable?"

"No!" He adored the look of mock shock on her face. "You're not available," she stated firmly.

Cocking her head to the side, she stared intently into his eyes. "Did you go to church on Sunday?"

"Lee and I went to services at the post chapel."

"You did? What did you think of it?"

Remembering the solemnness and the sense of peace filling the cool interior of the old stone chapel, he struggled to put his feeling into words. "It was strange to see so many men in uniform bowing their heads in prayer. I mean, these are America's warriors."

"And yet they seek a power greater than themselves."

They stopped beneath the towering branches of a cottonwood tree resplendent with bright yellow fall foliage. He studied her face turned so trustingly toward his. "It made me think about you and the way you face life with such confidence."

She blushed and looked down. "You make me out to be better than I am."

"No. I don't think so."

He caught sight of his sergeant motioning for him to return. Quickly, he said, "The American Cavalry Association always holds a reception and ball the night before the contest begins. Would you come with me as my date? I know it's short notice."

Her face brightened, but then she quickly frowned. "Do I have to wear a period ball gown? Because, I'd rather not."

He chuckled. "Modern dress is acceptable. Will you come? I wanted to ask you at the festival, but things got a little out of hand."

"Yes, they did, and I'd be delighted to go with you if my mother is doing okay. Thursday evening, right?"

"Right. Our unit is performing in Wichita that afternoon, so I might be a little late picking you up."

"What time does it start?"

"Nine o'clock in Wellford Hall."

"Why don't I meet you there?" she suggested.

"You don't mind?"

"Of course not. I'm perfectly capable of driving myself, and that way if I get mad at you for ogling other women, I can just leave."

"I'll never look at another woman except you," he said sincerely.

"Oh, I like the sound of that."

He brushed his knuckles along her cheek. "I wish I could spend more time with you, but I have to get back to work."

"I understand. Can I stay and watch? Friends

of my mother are sitting with her and the kids so I have a little time to myself."

"Sure. There are always a few people in the stands when we're here. I'd love to have you stick around."

Hand in hand, they walked back the way they had come. Jennifer said, "You know, I'm still your riding coach for a few more days. I'm going to be taking notes."

He laughed. "I'll be on my best behavior."

"Let me be the judge of that."

Still chuckling, he left her at the gate and re-mounted. The sergeant soon had them form up and begin practicing the drills they would be doing in the military horsemanship part of the cavalry competition. When Avery finished his turn, he caught Jennifer's eye. She gave him a thumbs up sign and he smiled.

Watching Lee go next, Avery noticed his friend's horse wasn't advancing freely and had trouble making the required gait changes smoothly. Avery nudged Dakota over to where Sergeant Stone sat on his horse. He said, "Lee is having a little trouble with Jasper."

Sergeant Stone glanced at Avery. "He's not as smooth as Dakota, that's for sure. Your riding has really improved. That should give you another leg up in the competition."

"I hope so."

The sergeant leaned forward in his saddle. "Most of us are pretty good troopers, but a lot of us, myself included, are counting on you to win the overall. Now, that doesn't mean I won't try my best to beat you."

After a moment of hesitation, Avery said, "I've had the benefit of a really good riding coach. She's here today. What would you say if I asked her to give everyone a few pointers?"

"I'd say that would lower your chances of winning the Sheridan Cup."

Avery smiled. "Not by much. I'm still the best."

"Then tell your coach we'd be happy to accept some pointers. There's also a prize for best unit performance and I'd like to win that one."

"I'll do my best to make it happen, Sarge."

Riding to the fence in front of where Jennifer sat on the edge of the bleachers, Avery said, "Jenny, how would you feel about giving the guys some tips?"

A wide smile lit up her face. "Are you kidding? I've been biting my fingers to keep from shouting corrections."

"I thought as much. Come on, the army can use a woman like you."

The night of the Cavalry Ball, Avery phoned to tell her he would be a few minutes late when

Jennifer was already on her way into Wellford Hall. Tucking her cell phone back in her purse, she continued up the steps of the building. She truly didn't mind. Spending the evening in his company once he arrived would be reward enough for her patience. Her relationship with Avery seemed to be the one thing going right in her life.

Her mother's surgery had gone well, but she would need more rehabilitation. Jennifer tried not to think about the mounting cost.

Without her mother's income, even the monthly bills would be hard to cover once Jennifer's savings were gone. She had asked for more hours at the clinic today, but Dr. Cutter wasn't able to promise them. There wasn't a full-time position available and poor students like herself were always eager for the part-time hours.

One thing was certain. Jennifer couldn't share any of her worries with her mother. The last thing she needed was her mother refusing needed treatment or drugs because she felt she was being a burden on her children.

"A penny for your thoughts."

Shaken out of her black cloud by the statement, Jennifer turned to look over her shoulder. "They aren't worth that much, Mr. Barnes."

Edmond, resplendent in a tuxedo, smiled at

her. "I think they're worth much more than that. Is my grandson here?"

"He's running a little late. I am surprised to see you here."

"I wanted to show my support. By the way, you look lovely, my dear."

"Thank you. It's last year's dress and I was worried I'd be out of date, but it seems I'm not the only one without a new gown." She glanced around at the numerous women in Victorian and Regency ball gowns. The men were all dressed in formal military attire from various periods in history with only a sprinkling of modern uniforms and an occasional tux.

Jennifer pressed a hand to her waist. "Avery said modern dress was acceptable, but he didn't tell me I'd be in the minority."

She looked down at her dress and hoped Avery would like it. A vibrant red, the gown had a front neckline that was modestly high, but the back had a daring low cut. The full skirt swirled about her legs when she moved but it was her red high heels that made her feel like a movie star.

"Beauty is never out of place," Edmond said with a slight bow. "Allow me to keep you company until my grandson tears you away."

"That's very kind of you, sir." She accepted his arm.

"Have you signed up for the competition? I understand the deadline has been extended until midnight tonight."

"Me? Why would I sign up?"

"For the prize money, of course. The purse is now ten thousand dollars for first place, with two thousand for second and a thousand for third place."

"You must be joking."

"I assure you I'm quite serious. You really should enter. I know you have the skills. I witnessed your daring ride on Saturday, and you handle a saber like a pro."

The possibility of paying her mother's medical bills and staying in school suddenly loomed in front of her like a very plump orange carrot. Then Avery's image took its place. She shook her head. "Avery is determined to win."

"The boy certainly doesn't need the money. Besides, I think the two of you might enjoy seeing who is the more skilled. It will make for an exciting match. Come, the registration table is set up in the back corner of the room."

She tilted her head toward him. "Are you the one who donated so much money?"

"I believe the Cavalry Association's benefactor stipulated that he or she remain anonymous."

"But I can guess."

"You may speculate all you wish." He patted the hand that rested on his arm. "My dear, you have brought about wonderful changes in my grandson. Because of you, I see him becoming the man I always hoped he would be."

"Avery isn't putty in my hands. He's his own man."

"Perhaps, but you have had a strong influence on him and all for the better. A few thousand dollars won't make a difference to me, but if someone needy should win the Sheridan Cup, then perhaps I will sleep better knowing I have done a good service, too."

"I don't know. Avery is very determined to win."

"Goodness, Miss Grant, you speak as if you two would be the only ones entering the event. I've been told there are over a hundred contestants so far."

Mr. Barnes was right. She wouldn't be the only one competing. If she won, it would be on her own merits, the same as every other rider. The prize money was so tempting. It would solve so many problems.

She made up her mind, ignoring the tiny

voice of caution in the back of her mind. "All right, Mr. Barnes. I accept the challenge. Show me where to sign up."

"Right over there." He pointed to the far corner of the room. "If you will excuse me for a few minutes, I see someone I'd like to speak with. I'll rejoin you shortly."

"Of course." Taking a deep breath. Jennifer made her way toward the registration table.

Avery spotted Jennifer across the crowded room and froze in his tracks. She looked absolutely breathtaking.

From the tips of her red high-heeled shoes to the elegant upsweep of her hair, she radiated poise and grace. The shimmering red dress she wore floated around her trim figure like the petals of some exotic orchid as she made her way between groups of people toward him.

But it wasn't her outfit or her hairdo that made him think she was the most beautiful woman in the room. It was the way her eyes lit up when she caught sight of him.

His heart kicked into overdrive when he realized the soft smile on her lips was meant for him alone. If he lived to be a hundred he would never forget how she looked tonight.

"She's a very attractive woman."

Avery spun around at the sound of his grandfather's voice. "What are you doing here?"

"I've discovered I have a passion for this cavalry business."

Avery allowed a small piece of hope to grow. Could it be that the two of them were going to find some common ground after all this time?

Jennifer reached Avery's side and slipped her arm through his. "Avery, I'm so glad to see you," she gushed.

He leaned to whisper in her ear. "You look gorgeous."

With a sparkle in her eyes, she replied, "You don't look half bad yourself. Formal military dress becomes you, but then I've always liked a man in uniform."

"Then I'll stay in one all my life."

"Are you planning to make the military your career?" Edmond asked.

Avery nodded. "I might."

Jennifer, bubbling with excitement, squeezed his arm. "Avery, you'll never guess what? Your grandfather has donated over ten thousand dollars in prize money to the cavalry competition."

Cocking his head to the side, Avery studied his grandfather's face. "Why would you do that?"

"It seemed like a worthy cause."

A sinking sensation settled in Avery's

stomach. "You did it to push up the number of competitors. With money like that at stake, every Tom, Dick and Harry will enter."

"And Henrietta," Jennifer added.

Avery frowned as he stared at her. "You plan to enter?"

"I just did. Are you worried?"

Edmond rocked back on his heels. "I saw her ride last weekend. I think she can beat you."

A chilling cold settled in the center of Avery's chest. What Edmond really meant was that Jennifer could humiliate him. His grandfather had found another way to use his money to drive a wedge between Avery and the woman he loved.

Reaching out, Avery gripped her arm. "Don't do it."

"What?" Her eyes widened with shock.

"Don't do it. Don't take his bait."

"What are you talking about?" She looked back and forth between the two men.

"He wants to make a fool out of me again."

Edmond shook his head. "You're wrong, Avery."

"Jennifer, don't fall for this. He wants to prove that money is more important to you than I am."

She shook her head. "Avery, don't be ridiculous. It's a contest. Anyone can win it. You could still win. In fact, I'm pretty sure you will."

"I'll give you ten thousand dollars not to ride."

Her mouth dropped open. "Why would you even suggest such a thing?"

"If it's money you want, why not take it from me?"

Disbelief, then sadness appeared in her eyes. "Because I'm willing to try and win fair and square. I'm not willing to accept a hand-out. I thought you knew me better than that."

"I don't care about your principles. I thought you knew how important this competition is to me."

"Apparently it's more important than our relationship."

He could see everything falling apart in front of his eyes and he didn't know how to stop it. He didn't dare look at his grandfather. He didn't want to see the triumph on the old man's face.

Tears glistened in her eyes, but she raised her chin. "If you gentlemen will excuse me, I'm going home."

Edmond placed a hand on her arm. "Miss Grant, please don't leave. This is my fault. Avery, tell her you don't want her to leave."

Avery clenched his hands into fists at his sides. *Pretend it doesn't matter. Don't give him the satisfaction of seeing how much this hurts.*

Only it did matter and it did hurt.

Jennifer pulled away from Edmond. "The fault is mine for expecting something different the second time around."

With that she hurried away through the crowd and out the doors.

Chapter Eighteen

Jennifer held back most of her tears until she reached home. Once inside her own bedroom, she gave into the pain. Throwing herself down on her bed, she clutched her pillow to her face and let loose the sobs building inside. She was so thankful her mother wasn't present to see what a wreck she had become.

Her mother wasn't home, but her hiccupping sobs, muffled as they were, brought Lizzie to her room.

"Jennifer, what's wrong? Has something happened to Mom?"

Shaking her head and embarrassed that she had worried her little sister, Jennifer managed to eke out a sentence, "Mom's fine—Avery's—a-a—jerk."

"Oh, no. What happened?" Lizzie sat beside her sister on the edge of the bed.

It took several long minutes, but Jennifer was finally able to control her sobs enough to sound coherent. Sitting up, she told Lizzie what had transpired between her and Avery.

"He actually offered you money to withdraw? What a chicken."

"He's not a chicken." She hiccupped once. "He just wants to win that stupid cup. He thinks it will prove something to his grandfather."

"What are you going to do?"

"Do you think I should withdraw? Not for the money, of course. Why he thinks everything hinges on money is beyond me."

"Duh!" Lizzie said. "Because he's always had it and we haven't."

"I thought he was beginning to see that other things are more important," Jennifer said sadly.

"Well, you can't withdraw. Even if you come in dead last you need to let him know that trying is as important as winning."

"I don't know. I signed up because I was greedy, too. The money would mean so much to this family."

"Yes, it would. Don't think the rest of us kids don't know how hard it's been on you and Mom."

"I'm looking for a job," Toby announced, stepping into the doorway.

"Me, too," Ryan said, worming his way in between his brother and the doorjamb.

Tears stung Jennifer's eyes again as she held out her arms. Toby and Ryan joined her and Lizzie in bed and they all held on to one another.

"I love you all," Jennifer whispered when she could speak past the lump in her throat.

"We love you, too," Ryan assured her. Wiggling out of his sister's embrace, he sat back. "You're gonna beat the pants off those army guys, aren't you?"

Jennifer ruffled his hair. "Do you think I can?"

"I think you can," Toby stated firmly.

Lizzie smiled. "If Henrietta Dutton could do it in a corset, girl, so can you."

Jennifer pulled them all into a hug again. "With a cheering section like you, I don't know how I can fail."

She managed to keep a smile on her face as she sent them all to bed. When she was alone again she sat on the edge of the bed and pulled off her shoes with a sigh. She had wanted to look beautiful for Avery tonight.

Wrapping the stilettos in tissue paper, she placed them back in their box and tucked them into the bottom corner of her closet. It would be a long time before she could wear them again without thinking of Avery and the heartbreak of this evening.

Avery stormed into his apartment, replaying every word he had spoken to Jennifer in his head. Throwing off his jacket, he flung himself down on his sofa. He wanted to be mad at her but couldn't get that look of disappointment in her eyes out of his mind.

The hurt went deep in his soul. Deeper even than Miranda's betrayal, because he hadn't loved Miranda the way he loved Jennifer.

He banged his fist into the arm of the couch. If only she loved him back.

Rising, he paced back and forth across the room. He knew she needed the money. It wasn't that he didn't want her to have it. If she loved him, why couldn't she put her scruples aside and accept it from him instead of falling in with his grandfather's backhanded attempt to bribe her?

"God, why did You let me fall in love with her?" he demanded, looking up.

The realization of what he was doing stopped him in his tracks. He was talking to God. Wasn't that what Jennifer said prayer was—just talking to God?

He ran his hands through his hair. *Do angry words count as prayers? Jennifer would know.*

Sitting down in the closest chair, Avery propped his elbows on his knees and dropped his head onto his hands. "I'm such a fool."

Jennifer was *who* she was because of her scruples, because of her beliefs. That was why he loved her.

That was why he had begun to question the life he'd led until now. Because she made him take a long hard look at himself and he didn't like what he saw.

Lord, I've turned away from people who cared about me because I was afraid of being hurt. I see now that I've hurt myself far more than others have hurt me.

Help me to trust, Lord. Help me to make amends. I know I don't deserve another chance with Jennifer, but I love her. I'm begging You. Help me find my way.

A thunderous pounding at his front door startled him. Then he heard his grandfather's voice shout, "Avery William Patrick Barnes, you open this door!"

"Great," Avery muttered. "This is just what I need."

The pounding started again. He rose and went to the door before his neighbors called the cops. He pulled it open to see his grandfather glaring at him. "We are going to speak, young man, and you are not shutting me out anymore."

Shaking his head in resignation, Avery motioned for him to come in.

Edmond looked slightly surprised, but marched in and spun around to face Avery. "You owe that young woman an apology."

Avery pushed the door shut. "That isn't exactly a newsflash, Grandpa. I've figured that out by myself."

"Oh. Well—good."

"Have a seat." Avery gestured toward the living room.

Edmond drew himself upright. "I prefer to say what I've come to say on my feet. I have never been ashamed of you, Avery. I have always loved you. I ignored you as a child, and that is my loss. I worked to accumulate wealth never knowing that the most important things in my life were slipping away.

"I apologize for the way I treated you, for the things I did and said that hurt you. There. That is all I wanted to say, except to ask that you forgive me."

Avery bit the inside of his lip to hold back the sting behind his eyes. "Would you like to sit down now?"

Edmond nodded and wiped at his eyes as he turned toward the sofa. Sinking into the cushion, he seemed to age before Avery's eyes.

Sighing, Edmond said, "I'm sorry about tonight. Miss Grant and her mother are genuinely caring people. I've come to know Mary well in the past two weeks and I like her a great deal. She is the oddest, most adorable woman I've ever met in my life, but she is very proud."

Avery couldn't keep the shock off his face. He sank into the chair across from his grandfather. "You were trying to help Mary Grant by putting the money up in the hopes that Jennifer could win it?"

Edmond nodded. "It wasn't the best of plans, but it was the only way I could think of that Jennifer might actually accept. Mary is heartbroken that her daughter has to drop out of school because of her."

Avery leaned back and stared at the ceiling. "We've made a mess of our lives, haven't we?"

"Indeed. I've made a fine mess of mine, but you are young and you have a chance to undo the mistakes you've made."

Avery laughed but there was no humor in it. "I broke her heart once because I was scared to death of loving someone. I broke her heart tonight because I want to prove to you that I was worthwhile, that I could excel at something and make you eat your words. Have you ever heard of such a stupid motive for driving away the woman you love? She isn't going to give me another chance."

Avery looked at his grandfather. "I owe you an apology, too. I tried to make your life miserable by my behaviors in the past. Can you forgive me?"

"I think we're both well on the way to forgiveness now."

Avery nodded. "Jennifer once told me that forgiveness heals the forgiver as well as the forgiven."

Edmond smiled. "She sounds like her mother. What are you going to do?"

Avery leaned forward and laced his fingers together. "I'm going to win her back."

"How do you plan to do that?"

"I have no idea."

"I hate to suggest this, but what if you withdrew from the competition?"

"Unfortunately, I have more to consider than my feelings for Jennifer. My commanding officer, the rest of the men in my unit, they're all counting on me to win the Sheridan Cup for Fort Riley. I can't let them down."

Chapter Nineteen

"He's coming," Lizzie hissed in Jennifer's ear the next morning. They were standing with a group of contestants outside the arena entrance waiting for the judges to allow them to walk through the jump course prior to the start of the first event.

The men and a few women around her were all dressed in reproductions of military uniforms ranging from a buckskin clad army scout to a World War I general. Since period clothing was one of the requirements for the competitors, Jennifer had borrowed a Civil War uniform from Gerard Hoover.

Jennifer kept her eyes forward. She wasn't sure she could keep from crying if she looked at Avery. She should have known trying to ignore him wouldn't work, because he walked up and stopped beside her.

"I'm glad to see you, Jennifer," Avery said quietly. "I wanted to wish you the best."

Struggling to hold on to her composure, she replied coolly, "The same to you."

Toby came marching up and stood toe-to-toe with Avery. "I told you if you ever made my sister cry again I'd knock your block off."

"Toby, please don't make a scene." Despite her words, Jennifer wanted to kiss her brave little brother.

"You would be well within your rights to blacken both my eyes," Avery said, surprising Jennifer.

"I could do it, too." Toby raised one fist.

"I wouldn't try to stop you, but I know it would embarrass your sisters."

Some of the anger faded from Toby's face. "Just so we understand each other."

"We do."

Jennifer glanced up to find Avery gazing at her intently. Her heart turned over just as she knew it would. He looked like he hadn't slept at all.

He managed a slight smile. "Jennifer, I humbly apologize for my behavior last night and I hope that you can find it in your heart to forgive me one day."

"That doesn't mean she's going to let you win today," Lizzie piped up.

"Yeah," Ryan added, holding on to Lizzie's hand.

Nodding once, Avery never broke eye contact with Jennifer. "I wouldn't expect anything less from her than her best. I won't give anything but my best in return."

She knew he was talking about so much more than the event they were about to start. She tried to harden her heart against the pull of his intensity, but couldn't.

She looked away. "Words come easily to you. It's hard to judge when you mean them."

"Then I'll let my actions do the speaking from now on."

The arena gates opened and a small, dark-haired woman in jeans and a blue sweatshirt came out with a clipboard. One by one she called off their names and sent them into the course.

Jennifer, happy to escape Avery's overwhelming presence, walked past the low jumps quickly. The course wasn't nearly as complex as the ones she faced at the shows she attended. This would be the easiest part of her day.

If she could keep her mind on what she had to do and not on her aching heart.

Lizzie was waiting with Lollypop outside the

gates when Jennifer finished her walk through. Shooting a narrow-eyed glare at Avery's back, Lizzie said, "He has a lot of nerve."

"He apologized. That says something for him." Jennifer mounted and turned her horse toward the gate.

Looking up at her, Lizzie frowned. "Don't tell me you're still soft on the guy."

"I wish I could say I wasn't."

Jennifer managed to keep her wits about her long enough to make a clean run through the jumping component of the day. Avery had a fault-free ride as well, but her time was two seconds faster than his. Fifteen other riders also managed to finish the course without faults including several men from the CGMCG, three riders from Fort Humphrey and two men from the Kansas National Guard unit. Jennifer wound up in third place behind Lee Gillis and the man dressed in buckskins.

Afterward, while they waited for the saber course to be set up, Jennifer joined her brothers and sister in the stands. The bleachers were only half full, which surprised her. She thought more spectators would have come to see such an unusual contest.

Instead of concentrating on the targets being laid out on the field, her eyes strayed constantly to the group of Union troopers seated below her that included Avery.

Had she been rash to rush away last evening instead of talking to him about his accusations? She had been so hurt that he thought she could be bought off. Now, in the light of day, she considered how it must have looked to him.

He had made it clear from the start that winning the Sheridan Cup was very important to him. It must have seemed to him that she didn't care about his feelings, only about the money.

When the announcer called the contestants to the field, she found herself between Avery and Lee in the line up. She smiled at Lee. "You had a great ride this morning."

He patted Jasper's neck. "This fellow is ready to rock and roll today. You did well, too."

The announcer called his name and Lee rode into the course. Jennifer watched as he made another great run, and her heart sank as his time came up on the display board. What was she doing here? These men did this every day. How could she hope to win?

"You should stop holding back, Jenny," Avery said from her other side.

"I wasn't holding back," she insisted. "I beat you, didn't I?"

How like him to try to annoy her when she had been almost ready to forgive him.

"A measly two seconds for a show jumper of your caliber? Either you're holding back or you're scared."

She pressed a hand to her chest. "I am not scared of competing against you."

"Okay, I'm just making sure you have the right attitude for this event."

"There is nothing wrong with my attitude."

The announcer called her name. She drew her saber and kicked Lollypop into motion. The mare responded with a burst of speed and Jennifer felt the satisfying thunk as her blade hit every target she passed while she wove in and out of poles, through a set of gates and over a series of jumps before she came flying across the finish line.

Looking up at her time, she grinned as she realized she had bested Lee by a full second.

She turned to look at Avery as she rode out of the arena. He was grinning from ear to ear. "I knew you could do it," he said, as he rode past her on the way to the starting line.

Ryan and Toby ran up to her. "Wow, you were awesome," Ryan said, his eyes shining with pride.

Jennifer looked over her shoulder to see

Avery charging into the first set of hurdles. "It helps if you have the right attitude," she admitted with a little smile.

Although Avery finished first in the saber class, Jennifer managed to hold on to fourth place. In the Mounted Pistol event, she finished tenth. By the end of the day, there was only the Military Horsemanship class to complete.

She and Lollypop moved through the required moves with ease. After she was finished, she watched with interest as the two riders from the National Guard unit finished impressive rounds, as well.

When it was Avery's turn, she noticed he looked almost nervous. As if he sensed her watching him, he looked her way. "Have fun," she mouthed, knowing he was too far away to hear.

A smile broke over his face and he touched the brim of his hat in a salute.

His ride was good. Not as good as hers, but good enough to earn him third place. When the overall scores for the day were announced, Jennifer was happy to see that she was among the top ten riders who would be going after the Sheridan Cup.

As she was loading Lollypop for the trip home, Avery and his group rode past on their way to the stables. He pulled up as the others went on. "You did well today, Jennifer. You should be proud of yourself."

"I had plenty of encouragement." She nodded toward her family already in the truck.

"They are a great bunch."

"I'm surprised your grandfather wasn't here today," she said, not wanting to leave and yet feeling foolish for wanting to stay.

"He was going to spend today at the hospital with your mother, but he plans to be here tomorrow."

That Edmond was the visitor Mary had assured Jennifer would stay and keep her company today came as a bit of a shock. It must have shown on her face.

"I was wrong about him," Avery said. "He's trying, but he doesn't always go about things in the right way." He tipped his hat. "I look forward to seeing you tomorrow."

As he rode away, Jennifer smiled to herself. She looked forward to seeing him again, too.

At ten o'clock the next morning, Avery found himself in a group of nine men and one woman drawing numbers for their position in the final test of cavalry skills. A single course had been laid out that encompassed jumping, saber and pistol use as men might have faced on a battle-field a hundred years ago.

Jennifer drew number two. He drew number ten. The good thing about that was he would know exactly what he needed to do in order to win when his time came. The bad part was that he would have to wait to ride. He wanted to get it over with.

As the group walked back to where the horses were waiting, he was surprised when Jennifer fell into step at his side. If only he could find a way to keep her there, close beside him.

"Are you nervous?" she asked, pressing a hand to her stomach. The anxious look in her eyes reminded him of the first day he handed her a saber. So much had happened since then that he couldn't believe it had been less than three weeks ago.

"You shouldn't be nervous. You'll do fine," he assured her.

She shot a look toward the stands where her family was sitting. He saw his grandfather seated a few feet away from them. "Will I do well enough to win?" she asked.

"Only God knows the answer to that," he said, quietly, wishing he could make it happen for her. Wishing he could hold her in her arms again.

"That is so true."

By now, they had reached the horses. He held her stirrup as she mounted. Looking up at her, he said, "Don't hold back."

"Do I need another attitude adjustment?" She smiled at him and it warmed his heart and gave him hope.

"No. Have fun, be safe."

"You, too."

Watching her gallop toward the starting area, he knew he would never love another woman the way he loved her.

The first rider up knocked down two rails on the jumps and missed two balloons with his pistol. As he left the field and Jennifer rode on, Avery found himself holding his breath, willing her to do well and praying for her success.

Charging into the course like a true trooper, she had the crowd on its feet cheering for her. Her ride was flawless until the final leg, the pistol range. She missed one balloon, but still managed a good time and he blew out a breath of relief.

When she rode back to his side, he could see the disappointment written on her face.

"Don't look so sad. It was a good run."

"Not good enough."

"You don't know that. Wait and see before you throw in the towel."

One by one, the following riders either failed

to hit more targets or finished in longer times. By the time the ninth rider was coming down the stretch, it was clear that Jennifer's score was going to keep her in first place.

Now it was Avery's turn.

He heard his buddies cheering him on and saw Captain Watson giving him a thumbs-up sign. He glanced at his grandfather in the stands and saw Jennifer's family watching intently. The weight of what lay ahead of him seemed almost too much to bear. He knew he could win.

"Don't hold back," Jennifer said, sitting quietly on her horse and staring at him. Her bright blue eyes were shining with deep emotion.

He spurred Dakota toward the starting line. The horse pranced sideways in anticipation of the coming dash. Avery looked over his shoulder to see Jennifer had one hand pressed to her lips and her eyes closed. Focusing his attention back on the course, he drew his saber and charged.

Dakota sailed over the jumps without hesitation, keeping close to the targets and giving Avery every chance to make good hits. Switching to his gun for the last leg, Avery knew his time was good and his run was perfect until Dakota stumbled slightly before the first balloon and Avery's shot went wide. The horse recovered himself and kept going as Avery took out the next three targets until only one remained.

He saw the white balloon coming up on his right, but time seemed to slow down as he swung the barrel of his pistol toward it. His finger tightened on the trigger. He fired as he flew past and time sped up again as he raced toward the finish line and Jennifer's shocked, joyful face.

As he pulled to a halt and dismounted, his buddies all came to slap him on the back and tell him he had done a good job, but he only nodded and headed toward the woman he loved.

Catching hold of Lollypop's reins, he stared up at Jennifer and tried not to show how afraid he was. "I know that I don't deserve another chance with you, but I want one."

She stared at him in disbelief. "You missed your last target on purpose. You let me win."

"Prove it."

Shaking her head, she frowned at him. "What will your captain say?"

"The Sheridan Cup didn't go to Fort Humphrey so he'll be thrilled. Besides, you're like one of us."

"It's not right," she protested.

He smiled. "It's perfect."

Lee came running up and skidded to a halt

beside them. "Did you hear that? They just awarded Dakota best overall horse. Congrats, Jennifer, you were awesome. They'll be giving out the trophies in a few minutes. We've still got a chance to win best overall unit. Come on, Avery, mount up."

"In a minute."

As Lee hurried away, Avery drew a deep breath and looked up at Jennifer. "Darling, I'm in love with you and you're in love with me. Say it."

Jennifer fought back the tears that blurred her vision. She honestly didn't know if they were tears of joy or apprehension. She wanted so much to love him but was she risking more heartache?

"If I say it, you can't break my heart again. I don't think I could stand it."

"I won't. Darling, I'm so sorry for the way I treated you in the past. I want to make it up to you. Tell me how."

"I need a man that I can count on when things get rough."

"I'll be that man."

Oh, how she wanted to believe him. "I need someone who values my faith. If you can't do that—if you can't give God a chance to come into your life—then there isn't any point in our trying to make this work."

"I don't know how to be worthy of a woman as strong as you are. Give me your sword."

"Why?"

"I don't want you armed when I do this."

"Do what?"

"This." He grasped her by the waist, pulled her out of the saddle and into his arms. Which was exactly where she wanted to be. When his lips covered hers, she thought her heart might break as it expanded with happiness.

When he pulled away at last, he touched her cheek softly with the back of his knuckle. "You could do a lot better than a man like me."

"I'll be the judge of that."

"I don't have anything to offer you that really matters."

"What really matters, Avery?"

"Fidelity, honor, commitment, faith."

"You said faith. Does faith truly matter to you? Don't say yes just because you think that's what I want to hear."

A frown put a crease between his brows. "My faith isn't as strong as yours. Praying, trusting Him—it's new to me. I'm taking some baby steps here, but I believe I'm heading in the right direction."

She smiled at him with all the love in her heart. "I believe you are, too."

"I didn't have a clue what faith meant until I saw you putting it into action in your everyday life. I love you so much, Jennifer."

"Oh, Avery, I love you, too."

He shook his head in disbelief. "I can't believe God feels that I'm worthy of you, because I'm not."

She tipped her head to the side. "I can work on that."

His shout of laughter caused some of the people passing by to stop and stare but Jennifer didn't notice them. She was busy being kissed again.

* * * * *

Dear Reader,

A Military Match turned out to be one of those books that was simply fun to write. Not only did I get to continue the story of Jennifer and Avery from my book, *The Color of Courage,* but in doing research for this story I was able to attend the National Cavalry Competition held at Fort Riley, Kansas, in 2007. What a treat! I saw first-hand the enthusiasm of men and women who were both active military and civilian re-enactors.

Much to my surprise, it wasn't all young people in the events. Men and women of all ages donned authentic uniforms from the Civil War era to World War I and rode out with sabers and pistols raised to showcase their skill, or sometimes just their love of the tradition. There was even a competitor from Australia who demonstrated "tent pegging" with a lance. Very cool.

In *A Military Match,* I wrote about a fictitious contest I called the American Cavalry Competition and gave the Sheridan Cup to the winner along with prize money. In reality, the U.S. Cavalry Association hosts the National Cavalry Competition each year. The winner of the Director's Cup has his or her name inscribed on a bronze trophy kept at the U.S. Cavalry

Memorial Research Library located at Fort Riley, Kansas. You can learn more about this organization by visiting their Web site at:

www.uscavalry.org.

There is no prize money awarded to the competitors. They participate to keep the spirit of the cavalry alive. I, for one, am glad they do.

Patricia Davids

QUESTIONS FOR DISCUSSION

1. In what way does the scene at the beginning of the book—when Jennifer is trying to avoid meeting Avery—set the tone for the story?

2. What elements of Avery's character are revealed in the course of the story that are not seen in the first chapter?

3. Jennifer and Avery seem to be two people with very little in common. He makes no secret of the fact that he doesn't respect her faith. Have you or someone you know been belittled for your faith? How would you respond?

4. Even though Jennifer wants to avoid being involved with Avery, she still tries to help repair his relationship with his grandfather. Have you tried to help people at odds with each other mend their relationship? What was the outcome?

5. It took a crisis of health for Edmond Barnes to begin seeking a reconciliation with

Avery. Was he wrong to withhold his state of health from his grandson?

6. Isabella the rabbit is a character that drastically changes the course of Jennifer's life. Do you, or someone you know, own a pet that has altered their life? In what way?

7. How did the humor in this book add to your enjoyment of the story? What was your favorite scene and why?

8. Jennifer gives in to her mother's pleading to make the ride up Dutton Heights but finds it involves much more than she bargained for. When we agree to help others, we sometimes resent the demands placed upon our time and energies. How does our faith help us deal with those feelings?

9. What was the nature of the conflict between Avery and his grandfather? Do you think being wealthy makes it harder to trust others? Why or why not?

10. Mary Grant had an obsession with a personality from an earlier time period. Have you visited a place where living historians

re-enact the past? What is the draw of learning about history from such people?

11. Avery harbors a deep respect for the army and the men he serves with. In your opinion, does military service conflict with our faith as Christians?

12. What roles did Jennifer's siblings play in the story? How did they hinder and/or advance the development of their sister's romance?

13. Was Avery right to allow Jennifer to win the competition and the money she needed? Why or why not?

14. Would you plan a visit to watch a cavalry competition near you after reading this story? Is it important for the army to keep the tradition of the cavalry alive? Why?

Love Inspired®
SUSPENSE
RIVETING INSPIRATIONAL ROMANCE

Watch for our new series of
edge-of-your-seat suspense novels.
These contemporary tales
of intrigue and romance
feature Christian characters
facing challenges to their faith...
and their lives!

**Steeple
Hill**®

Visit:
www.SteepleHill.com